I0641289

Just Friends

AE Moran

Invisible Publishing Company

Contents

Chapter 1: Quinn

"**M**om—heads up!" My eight-year-old son Kai pivots on one foot and sends the frisbee soaring across the park. It makes a perfect arc and comes straight to my hand.

"Good shot, buddy!" my best friend Jayden Aldrich yells from the other side of the lawn.

I wing the frisbee back to Jayden, who catches it between both hands.

"Mom!" Kai bellows. "We're playing ultimate frisbee! Jayden is on the other team! You just handed the frisbee to the enemy."

I laugh and Jayden joins in. "Leave me out of the game, then, pal," I reply. "I don't even know how to play ultimate frisbee."

"You are so out of date, Mom," Kai informs me.

"You tell her, buddy!" Jayden calls and sends the frisbee gliding across the park.

Just then, a puff of wind carries the frisbee far to the right where Kai can't catch it no matter how hard he runs.

It lands at the edge of some trees far away from the lawn where he and Jayden have been playing and Kai stops to pick it up. Some other boys his age come out of the trees right at that moment and they start talking to him.

Jayden and I both watch him, but when Kai doesn't come back and then runs off with the boys and starts playing ultimate frisbee with them instead, Jayden saunters over to me. "It looks like we lost him. It's the beginning of the end."

"I know he likes you better and you're his big brother and all, but could you not make it so obvious that you're turning my son against me?"

He laughs and his green eyes twinkle when he smiles at me. He flips his long hair out of his eyes with that characteristic jerk of his head that he always uses. He started growing it out nine years ago when his wife left him and he refuses to cut it. It's his badge of defiance against the dating world even though long hair makes him look even better.

"What's the matter?" he teases. "You can't hang with the big boys. Sorry, darling, but you're bound to lose him someday. If it isn't me, it will be someone else like those boys over there."

"I know, but I'd like to think of him as my baby boy just a little longer."

Jayden puts his arm around my shoulder and gives me a quick hug. "You've done a fantastic job of raising him on your own since Max died. I thought you'd cave and find yourself a rich husband by now. You really knocked it out of the park by staying loyal to the Singles' Club."

I snort. "Very funny. Hey, speaking of which, will you go with me to my sister Karina's wedding? It's next Sunday at Lakewood Estates. If you don't come with me, my mom will try to set me up with someone she thinks would be a suitable match for me and he'll try to turn it into a real date."

Jayden laughs again. "Your mom really hasn't gotten the memo yet, has she?"

"Oh, she got it. She just ignored it—just like the other five hundred times."

"She should get together with my family," he replies. "They could talk about who they want us to hook up with instead."

"*You* don't have any trouble hooking up, Mr. Fly-By-The-Seat-Of-My-Pants. You hook up all the time. That's your problem."

"There's nothing wrong with my pants." He elbows me and roars with laughter. Then he gets serious. "No, really. My mother and my sisters are way worse than your mother and your sisters."

"So now we're competing to see whose family is worse? Don't they get that you don't want to repeat the disaster of Helena leaving you? She vanished in the middle of the night, emptied your bank accounts, and didn't even leave a note. Who would want to take the chance of that happening again? I can't decide which is worse—that or Max dying when we had just adopted a baby boy."

"Hey, at least I didn't get stuck with a kid for the rest of my life."

"Watch it!" I counter. "Kai is the best kid on the planet. Don't you dare say anything bad about him."

"You're right. He's an outstanding kid. You know it and I know it and we all know it. I really appreciate you letting me hang out with you. I get my family fix from you two while I keep playing the field. You ensure that I'm not tempted to settle down with anyone."

"Great," I grumble.

"So in answer to your question, yes, I will go with you to Karina's wedding."

"Thanks. I appreciate you taking one for the team."

"Team Single," he adds and we both laugh.

"And I don't *let* you hang out with me and Kai," I go on. "You make it sound like you're a charity case or something. You've been my best friend for as long as I can remember and I couldn't have done any of this without your support. You're my rock."

"Aw—baby!" He hugs me around the shoulders again and kisses me on the side of the head. "I love you, too."

"So who's your latest conquest?" I ask while we stroll across the lawn to where Kai disappeared. I don't hold out much hope of finding him until he gets hungry and comes home on his own, but it's nice just walking around talking to Jayden.

"I think her name was Abby or Tabby or Scabby or something. I can't remember. I don't seem to be able to stay interested in them for more than a few days. They all blend together after a while."

"You are such a clod. You know that, right?"

"I know, but at least I'm being true to myself. I don't lead these women on. I tell them from the beginning I'm not interested in anything more than a few days of fun. It isn't like I'm using them or anything."

"I think what you mean is that you're using them and they're using you."

"Whatever. It works. Just promise me you won't leave the Singles' Club. I need someone to commiserate with."

"Don't worry. I don't think I'll ever date again—definitely not until Kai leaves home. Losing Max was too painful. He was my high school sweetheart and going through all the medical problems he had at the end really took a lot out of me. I might not even go back to dating after Kai moves out. I don't know. I don't know if I can ever get over that, but I guess anything is possible."

"I don't blame you," he replies. "Besides, what we have now works so well. Why change it?"

"You're right. I feel the same way."

A yell interrupts our conversation and Kai comes tearing out of the woods with the other boys. "Mom—Tom's dad is barbecuing hot dogs and he invited me over. Can I go?"

"Okay," I reply. "Just show me where it is so I know where you are." I turn to Jayden. "I better go."

"All right, sweetie. I'll see you Sunday." He kisses me on the forehead again. "See you later, buddy!"

"Bye, Jayden!" Kai waves and then runs off. I wave to Jayden as he heads off across the park.

He's such a good friend and the best thing about him is that he never demands anything else. He just hangs out with me and Kai, supports us, and he never pushes the relationship to be anything more than it is.

I love having a man in Kai's life and they couldn't be closer. In a way, Jayden gives me something not even a real relationship could. He gives me totally unconditional support with no obligations or pressures. He's right. It's the perfect arrangement for everyone.

I don't relate to his need to leave a trail of hookups in his wake, but who am I to judge? Helena really cut him off at the knees and he's never heard from her since. In a way, losing her was worse for him than Max's death was for me. At least I know Max is dead and isn't coming back.

Helena is running around out there in the world. Jayden doesn't know where she is or what she's doing or when she might fall out of the clear blue sky to wreck his life a second time.

He really pulled it together after she left, too. We don't talk about it because he'd rather leave those dark days in the past. She left him penniless, but he dragged himself out of the mud and now he's running one of the biggest, richest, most successful firms in the country. He built his company from zero with no help from anyone.

I wouldn't want to risk someone taking all that away from me and he has plenty of experience after Helena did it to him once. He doesn't want to chance it happening again with someone else.

The problem is that most women in town already know who he is. They all want to date him because he's so rich and.... well.... he's hot. He's my best friend so I could never think of him that way, but even I have to admit that he's downright stunning.

He always attracts women who want his money. No wonder he loses interest in them.

I don't care. Let him have his fun. He'll always be in my life and him being a player doesn't affect how he acts around me and Kai. Jayden is great with Kai and he's never treated me with anything but respect and support.

Chapter 2: Jayden

I stick my head into Quinn Brown's apartment. "Hey, Quinn? You ready to go?"

No one answers me so I go right in. I open the fridge and take out a bottle of juice when Kai comes downstairs dressed in a very spiffy black suit with a black silk bowtie.

"Hey! Looking good, buddy!" I tell him. "You'll be knocking the girls dead dressed like that."

He turns bright red and squirms. "You don't look too bad yourself."

I shrug the jacket of my tux into place and turn from one side to the other like the stud I am. "What do you think? Do you think I could get picked up as the next James Bond?"

He laughs. "James Bond doesn't have long hair."

"That's his mistake. Where's your mom?"

"Still upstairs getting ready."

I stick my head up the stairs and yell, "Quinn! It's time to go! You're gonna be late!"

"I'm coming!" she calls from out of sight.

I turn back to Kai. "And she was never seen or heard from again."

He laughs again. "I don't think we could get away with that. She's always around."

"She's a good mom. She would never leave you alone."

I sit down at the kitchen counter to drink my juice and he comes over to lean against the counter. "Could I start learning about your company, Jayden?"

"What do you want to learn about my company for? You said you were interested in engineering. You don't want to get locked up in the corporate world."

"You're rich."

"So what? Being rich isn't all it's cracked up to be. Look at your mom. You guys aren't rich and you have more than I do."

"No, we don't. You have a much nicer car."

"So? Do you think life suddenly gets better because you have a better car? Look at this place." I wave at the apartment. "You have everything you want. You don't need money."

He shuffles his feet and looks away. "All the boys at school want to be as rich as you."

"I'd like to see them try it for a week. They wouldn't like it near as much, but if you really want to learn about my company, you can."

His face lights up. "Really? You would do that?"

"Sure. If you learn about it, you'll find out pretty quick that being an engineer is way more interesting. If I had to do it over again, I would probably become an engineer."

"But engineers don't make as much money as you do."

I study the kid in front of me. I could tell him all about why being an engineer is better than having a bunch of money. Helena wouldn't have left me in pieces if I didn't have money, but Kai is too young to understand that.

He doesn't understand how much I regret marrying her. If I knew then what I knew now, I would have smelled a gold digger a mile away. I would have realized she was never interested in anything but my money, and as soon as she got that, she hit the bricks and took all my money with her.

If I had been working as a humble engineer, I would have married someone who just wanted to live a normal middle-class life instead of riding high on the hog all the time. I would be living in the suburbs with my boring wife and kids and paying a mortgage and that would be it. Every gold digger in town wouldn't be trying to hook up with the rich big-shot Jayden Aldrich.

I'm just trying to figure out how to explain even half of this to Kai when Quinn comes downstairs. She looks magnificent in a full-length white dress studded with pale cream silk flowers. The dress really shows off her figure and the scattering of the same silk flowers in her curly chestnut hair sets off the sparkle in her turquoise eyes.

I stand up and grin at her. "You look outstanding—almost good enough to be the bride."

She blushes. "Don't let Karina hear you talking like that. She's already jealous enough as it is."

"Maybe if she took better care of herself, she'd have less to be jealous about."

She bites back a grin and her cheeks flush even darker. She's gorgeous. It's a good thing she's so dedicated to staying single or some lucky bastard would have snapped her up years ago.

"Don't talk like that at the wedding, okay? Please." She rummages in her handbag and then turns to Kai. "You look nice, too, sweetie."

"You didn't say I look nice, sweetie," I tell her and make her laugh.

"You don't need some girl telling you that you look nice," she tells me. "Your head is already way too big."

Kai punches me hard in the shoulder. "She burned you so bad, dude!"

"Watch it, kid," I tell him. "You don't want to get into a burn competition with me."

"Are you ready to go?" Quinn interrupts.

"I've been ready to go for ten minutes. I've been waiting for you."

"Okay. I'm ready. Come on, Kai."

We go outside, get in my car, and drive across town to the Lakewood Estates. I pull up in front of the entrance and hand my eyes to the valet before I turn to Quinn and stick out my elbow. "Shall we make them think we're on a real date?"

"You're so bad."

"Come on. You know you want to. Make them think we're a couple."

She laughs and Kai joins in. "Go on, Mom. Everyone wants to date Jayden."

"I don't," she counters. "How do you know about that, anyway?"

"Tom's aunt and sister were talking about it at the barbecue at the park. They saw me talking to Jayden and then they started talking about how he always...."

"I don't want to hear it!" Quinn holds up her hand and turns her head away. "We aren't here to talk about Jayden's dating life."

"We aren't?" I ask and get another laugh from Kai.

Quinn tries to give me a dirty look and winds up grinning. "No, we're here for a wedding. Now come on."

I stick out my elbow at her again and she blushes and takes it. There. Now I'll have the most beautiful woman at this wedding on my arm and we aren't even dating. I can just imagine what her mom will say when she sees us showing up together. Mrs. Brown has been trying to set me up with Quinn for decades.

We walk into the club and out onto the terrace. The whole terrace, garden, and the huge lawn is set up for the wedding with a giant marquee, acres of buffet tables with plenty of ice sculptures, and a hundred people milling around in fancy clothes.

Kai runs off with some other kids and Quinn's friend Harper Murdoch comes sweeping over to her. Harper grabs Quinn's other arm. "You HAVE to come over and see Karina's dress, Quinn! It's spectacular!"

"I've seen it," Quinn replies.

Harper glances over at me and blushes. "Hi, Jayden."

I say, "Hello," as politely as I can, but I would have to be blind not to see Harper shooting me the side-eye. She's been doing that a lot lately. Hey, if she wants to wind up on the scrap heap with Abby, Tabby, and Scabby, who am I to argue?

Quinn pretends not to see Harper eyeing me. Quinn is used to that after almost twenty years of friendship. We were friends as kids and we stayed friends all the way through the whole Helena disaster.

Now she's seen me hook up with I don't know how many girls. Quinn knows the drill. She might razz me about it sometimes, but she never judges. That's what's so great about her. She just accepts me for what I am without trying to change me into something else.

Speaking of which, I spot Quinn's mom coming toward us and I squeeze Quinn's arm. "I'm gonna go hit the booze. Do you want anything?"

She grins at me on the side. "That's right. Go hide at the bottom of a bottle."

"I'll need it to deal with all the comments I'm about to get. See you later."

I split off and Harper drags Quinn off somewhere. I head for the nearest bar, but Quinn's mom intercepts me anyway. "Hi, Jayden!" she shrills.

"Hi, Mrs. Brown. How are you?"

"I'm wonderful! How are you? How's the dating scene these days?" She sure doesn't waste any time.

"I don't know. I don't date."

"Are you sure you didn't come as Quinn's date?"

"I came as her date for this wedding, but we aren't dating. Sorry, Mrs. B. I wish I could tell you otherwise."

"When are you going to settle down with someone? You're so successful. You could find a nice girl...."

"I'll work on it. Thank you."

I take my drink from the bartender, pound it, put the glass down, and point into it so he gives me another one. Quinn's mom has been on my case for decades to get married. She doesn't know or doesn't want to believe that I'm still legally married to Helena and I don't want to get mixed up with anyone else.

I could tell her that all day every day for the next fifty years and she still wouldn't believe it. I can just imagine the hints and suggestions Quinn is getting from her sisters and Harper behind my back. They've been after Quinn for years to remarry and they don't listen to her any better than they listen to me. They don't understand why she might actually want to raise her son alone.

Quinn's mom makes me stiffen by squeezing my arm. She leans in close and almost whispers in my ear even though the bartender can hear her perfectly well. "You and Quinn have always been close. Why don't you take it to the next level?"

"I don't think so, Mrs. B. We're just friends. You know that."

Of course she knows it. God only knows why she keeps dropping these remarks every time we see each other.

"A man and a woman can't be friends," she tells me. "Someone always wants something more. It's a law of nature."

Okay, now I know I absolutely HAVE to end this conversation. I turn to face her and level her with an unwavering stare. "Have you ever heard Quinn say that she wants to date me? Have you ever heard her say that even once? Has she ever, in all the years we've known each other, even once mentioned taking our friendship to the next level?"

"Well, no, but ......"

"Then there's your answer. She doesn't want to date me, so that's the end of it."

I turn back to the bartender and take my third drink. Of course Quinn doesn't want to date me. She's my best friend. We're practically brother and sister. We're too close and neither of us wants to date anyone anyway.

Mrs. Brown finally gets the message. She leaves, but not before she squeezes my arm and says, "If you ever want me to set you up with someone, you let me know."

"You'll be the first person I call if I need any help finding a date, Mrs. B," I tell her.

She takes off and I groan into my drink. It's going to be a long afternoon. Quinn's mom would be the absolute last person I would ever ask to set me up with someone. I shudder to think what kind of woman she thinks would be a good match for me.

She doesn't know about my string of conquests. She couldn't possibly know if she suggested setting me up with someone. She wouldn't want to throw another respectable girl into the meat grinder.

I turn around nursing my drink and see Quinn across the lawn with Harper and Quinn's other sister, Sandy. Quinn doesn't look happy. Maybe I should rescue her.

I stroll over there and Harper and Sandy get all stupid when I ease in and stand next to Quinn. Harper can't stop falling over herself smiling at me and Sandy blushes and doesn't say a word.

I take Quinn's elbow and steer her away. "How's it going?"

"Why did I agree to come to this wedding?" she murmurs under her breath.

"Because the bride is your sister."

"Oh, right. I forgot."

"That bad, huh?" I ask.

She nods. "One of these days, someone is going to invent a mechanized robot that looks lifelike enough to pass for human. I'll get one to bring to these events so everyone thinks I have a boyfriend—or a husband."

"Maybe I should invent one. I could make a mint."

She shoots me a grin. "I thought you were one. I thought you could act as a stand-in so no one would ask too many awkward questions."

"Let me guess. They want to hook us up with each other."

"How did you know?"

"Your mom just ambushed me by the bar."

She covers her eyes and groans. "God Almighty! That was fast."

"Let's go sit down in the marquee. It's empty. We can hide from everyone in there."

We go sit down in front of the altar and talk for a while. I realize too late that this makes it look even more like we're involved, but whatever. Everyone already thinks that, so why not?

Fortunately, we're in a perfect position when people start entering the marquee for the ceremony. We don't have to go anywhere and no one drops any hints....yet.

We get through the ceremony just fine and then lunch starts. I sit next to Quinn and Kai sits on her other side at the table. We're isolated enough from everyone until after lunch.

The instant we stand up, some executives of another company that rents a building I own come over to talk to me. Quinn gets swept into another conversation nearby with Harper and some of their other female friends.

I'm talking business not thinking anything of it when loud laughter makes me glance over my shoulder. The world comes to a screeching halt when I see a bunch of guys gathered around Harper, Quinn, and her friends.

One of the guys dives in and kisses Quinn on the cheek and then, right in front of me, he puts his arm behind her and places his hand on her back.

I wouldn't normally care about some yahoo hitting on her, but she visibly recoils from the guy and tries to move away from him. She shakes his arm away, and the very next second, he takes a step forward and does the same goddamn thing.

She spins around to confront him. I can't even hear what they're talking about, but the body language is unmistakable. She doesn't like this creep and I see the whole disaster winding up to blow.

I walk away from the business conversation and shove between Quinn and the guy. I break in on them so suddenly that he winds up putting his arm around me for a split second before he realizes that I'm there.

"You can see she isn't interested in you, buddy," I tell him. "Keep your hands to yourself."

The dude squares his shoulders and looks me up and down. He's at least four inches taller than me, but if he's messing with Quinn, that won't help him. "Who the hell are you?" he snaps.

"I'm the guy that's taking her home after this so back your ass right off before you get taken home in an ambulance. She already pushed you away once, and if you don't get the message, I'll do it for her."

"Who are you—her boyfriend?" The guy takes a threatening step toward me and bumps his chest into mine. "You forgot to cut your hair for the last ten years."

"I didn't forget how to behave in public." I cock my head and study him. "I recognize you. You're a broker with Emery & Banrock, aren't you?"

The guy stiffens visibly. "Who's asking?"

"Jayden Aldrich—that's who." The temperature drops by twenty degrees as the penny drops. Dead quiet falls over the group of idiots standing behind this chump.

"You've got some growing up to do in your chosen profession if you don't even recognize your own company's major investors," I go on. "If I was you, I'd take your boys here and go back to the office for the rest of the weekend before someone decides to make a few phone calls about your behavior."

The guy stands his ground for another half a second before one of his friends takes his arm and saves his face by pulling him away.

I stay where I am until they disappear into the crowd. Then I turn around to find Quinn cowering behind me. "You okay?" I ask her.

She nods quickly and her eyes dart around the tent. Dozens of eyes watch us talking. "Thanks," she murmurs.

"You've been holding out on us, Quinn," one of her friends comments. "You didn't tell us you and Jayden were seeing each other."

"We aren't seeing each other," I tell her. "We're friends. How many times do we have to tell you?"

"You could have fooled me," Harper replies. "You're sure acting protectively of her if you're just friends."

I smack my lips in exasperation, but I don't dignify these remarks with an answer. It's all we ever hear whenever we go to any family function together. It's nothing new, but it doesn't get any easier.

I take Quinn's elbow and pull her away. "Come over here and sit down."

Harper and her friends giggle behind their hands as we walk away, but Quinn doesn't. She passes her hand across her forehead. She's looking pale.

I pull her down into one of the empty chairs at the lunch tables. "Do you want to go home?" I ask her. "We can get out of here if you've had enough of this."

"I wish I could, but I have to stay for Karina. We're supposed to take a bunch of family photos right before she leaves for her honeymoon."

"Well, just stick close to me. You don't have to walk around socializing with everyone." I look over at her and see her sweating bullets. "Are you sure you're okay?"

"That guy...." she starts to say and breaks off by compressing her lips. I haven't seen her this disturbed in a long time.

"Don't worry about it," I tell her. "He was a moron."

"Thanks for intervening. I wasn't sure if I could handle it."

"You shouldn't have to. You have enough to deal with without fighting off jackasses like that. He needed someone to straighten him out."

She smiles, but not very convincingly.

"Do you want something to drink?" I ask her. "You don't look so good."

"I'm okay. I'm just....my heart is racing. I haven't had to deal with something like that since.... since before Max."

"I'll get you something to drink. Stay here." I look around the tent. I can see the bar from here, but I don't want to leave her alone.

I want to find someone to keep an eye on her while I'm gone, but Harper and the others are making such stupid faces across the tent that

I don't dare to leave. They'll swoop in and start filling her ears with their nonsense the instant I walk away.

Fortunately, at that moment, Kai and some other kids come into the tent on their way somewhere else. I grab him. "Hey, buddy! Sit down here and take care of your mom for a second. I'm going to get her a drink."

I push him into my chair and he turns to Quinn while I go to the bar. I check over my shoulder just to make sure they're talking before I walk away. I'll get her this drink and then I won't let her out of my sight until it's time to leave.

I might not be here as her real date, but no one is going to mess with her as long as I'm around. I don't need to be her boyfriend to take care of her.

Chapter 3: Quinn

My friend Harper Murdoch stretches out on my bed with her head dangling off the mattress and swipes her finger across her phone screen. She flips through all the photos from Karina's wedding. "Have you ever seen such a beautiful wedding dress? I'm going to get married in a dress just like that."

"You might want to find the guy first," I call from the other side of my bedroom. I keep folding laundry while we talk.

"It isn't from lack of trying. Oh, my God! Did you see her bouquet? Wasn't it stunning? All the flowers were to die for."

"Yeah, they were nice. The whole wedding was nice."

"Nice!" Harper yells and flips onto her stomach. "It was better than nice. It was dreamy. It was like a fairy tale."

"Well, maybe not as nice as that. The marquee was kinda stuffy. I liked Sandy's wedding better."

"You would find something wrong with any wedding," Harper grumbles. "You're a robot, Quinn."

"I'm not a robot. I'm just not as much of an airhead as you are. A wedding isn't an excuse to take leave of my senses. It's just another day."

"It was your sister's wedding day! No wonder Karina didn't choose you as one of her bridesmaids."

I snort and pick up the laundry basket. "She didn't choose me as one of her bridesmaids because she wanted her two best friends from grade school to be her bridesmaids instead."

I head off down the hall and down the stairs to the living room to put the laundry away. Harper jumps up and follows me downstairs talking fast.

"You could have at least stood by the altar with her instead of sitting in the seats like a total stranger. I don't understand you at all, Quinn. Where's your sense of romance?"

"My sense of romance died with Max and me standing next to Karina has nothing to do with romance. I've explained this to you a thousand times. James and Karina were the ones who decided who would stand where and who would be involved in the ceremony. It had nothing to me."

"I'll never believe that." She flops on the couch and starts scrolling through the pictures again. "What woman wouldn't want her sister standing by her on her wedding day?"

"Karina," I reply and start putting the clean dishtowels away in the kitchen, the clean bedding in the hall closet, and hanging up Kai's school clothes by the front door.

"I'm going to have my sisters as my bridesmaids," she tells me.

"I'm happy for you. When's the big day?"

"Stop it, Quinn!" she yells. "You're cruel."

"Hey, you don't see me getting married, either. We can be old maids together."

"You're marrying Jayden, aren't you?"

My head shoots up, but I relax when I see her smirking at me. "Don't start that again," I tell her.

"Oh, come on!" She comes over and leans across the kitchen counter to leer at me. "You can't tell me he wasn't acting protectively at the wedding."

"We're friends and that guy was acting like a jerk. Of course Jayden was acting protectively."

"You know it's more than that. Didn't you see the way he was hovering around you? He must have feelings for you."

"No, he doesn't. Jayden doesn't have feelings for anyone, especially not me. He considers me his little sister."

"I bet you he doesn't."

I groan and roll my eyes. "Whatever. You're as bad as my mom and Sandy."

"Maybe we all see something you don't. Why don't you go out with him? He's so rich and soooooooooo hot!" She puffs out her cheeks and waves her hand like she's fanning her face.

"Uh-huh. Tell me something I don't know."

"Ah-ha!" She points at me. "So you admit that he's hot!"

"Of course he's hot. That doesn't mean I want to date him. He's my oldest friend and he's been the one who's supported me ever since Max died. Jayden is like an uncle to Kai and...."

"Then he'd be perfect for you. You're already friends. Just take it to the next level and call it good."

"I wouldn't go out with Jayden even if he was interested in me—which he isn't. He's a player. You know that as well as I do, Harper. He fools around with a girl for two or three days and then gets bored and dumps her."

"He's got to stop playing the field someday. One of these days, he'll find someone who doesn't bore him and he'll settle down. He's the heir to the Aldrich fortune as well as being stinking rich in his own right. Why shouldn't he stop being a player with you? You'd be set for life if you bagged him."

"I don't want to bag him," I counter. "Why don't you go out with him if you think he's such a catch? I see you flirting with him every time you see him."

"Maybe I will."

I snort. "Good luck with that. Let me give you a piece of advice as your friend. Don't go near him unless you want a broken heart."

"Why shouldn't I flirt with him? He's so attractive and smart, and if he acted that way around you, he would be the territorial type with any woman he got serious with. That kind of alpha male protective behavior is soooooo hot!"

"Listen to me, Harper. I've known Jayden for years, and if there is one thing he cannot stand, it's a woman who wants him for his money."

"I never said I wanted him for his money. I said he was hot."

"You just said anyone he gets together with him will be set for life. You said he's the heir to the Aldrich fortune. He can smell that kind of attitude a mile away. He'll play with you and throw you away. Don't even go there. Trust me."

"You're only saying that because that's what he's done with every other girl he's ever met—except for his ex-wife, of course."

I don't correct her by pointing out that Jayden is still legally married to Helena. Not many people know about that little detail. Jayden can't get a divorce from Helena when he doesn't know where she is.

Harper won't listen to reason on anything else Jayden-related, so why should she listen to me about that? "And you think you're the exception?" I ask her. "You think you're the one woman in the world that he won't throw you away? You're crazy. You're cruising for trouble."

"I could be cruising for the man of my dreams. If you're really just friends with him, you shouldn't care if I go out with him."

"I care because I don't want you to get hurt. I know you too well. You'll get your heart broken and then you'll come crying to me about how Jayden dumped you."

"No, I won't."

I snort again. I've been the recipient of too many of Harper's tears after her dating disasters go wrong. This one promises to make the Mount St. Helens eruption look like a tea party if she really thinks she can make Jayden change his ways.

Chapter 4: Jayden

"I brought beer!" I set a twelve-pack on Quinn's coffee table, collapse on the cushions, and kick my feet up on the table. "Don't ever invite me to a wedding again, sweetie. Seriously. I'm not cut out for them."

She laughs and shoots me a grin from the desk in the corner where she works on her computer. "You and me both. I only went because my sister was the bride. I wouldn't have if I didn't think I would have to suffer biblical consequences if I skipped out."

"You aren't drinking." I take a beer from the box, carry it to her desk, and set it by her computer before I return to the couch. "We need to work our way through this whole box to drown the memory of last Sunday."

"Thanks, babe." She twists off the cap, takes a swig, and goes back to tapping on her keyboard. "How many times did my mom ambush you about hooking you up with someone?"

"Only four altogether. How many for you?"

"Only three from my mom. Sandy was in full battle mode, though....and don't even get me started on Harper."

"Did you tell Harper about my terrible reputation with women?" I ask.

She looks up. "Excuse me? Why are you asking me that?"

"I just wondered because she's always throwing herself at me and making eyes at me. I didn't think it was possible that a woman could be friends with you without you giving them the dirt of my evil ways."

She laughs again. "You're right. I did tell her, but I didn't have to because she already knew about you."

"She does?" I shrug. "Okay."

She gives me a knowing look and turns back to the screen. She doesn't mention Harper again and neither do I. Harper can't be very bright if she's still flirting with me after what she must have heard about me in this town.

Quinn taps a few more times and then a notification comes up on her phone which sits next to her on the desk. She glances at it and then reads the message. "Damn it."

"What's wrong?" I ask. "Did you get another wedding invitation—or did your admirer from Emery & Banrock propose marriage now that I'm not around to knock his teeth out?"

She doesn't take the joke. She starts clicking on her mouse and cursing under her breath. "Damn it, damn it, damn it. Did I say damn it? If that doesn't work, what are we supposed to try next?"

"What are you doing?" I ask again. "If what doesn't work?"

"I hired a private investigator to try to track down Kai's birth parents. The guy has been up and down the West Coast three times and he keeps striking out."

"What do you want to know that for?" I ask. "Kai is legally yours. Who his parents are doesn't matter."

"I know he's mine, but who his parents are *does* matter. I want him to know where he came from. He might have family somewhere or he might belong to a culture that will become important to him when he's older. The foster system didn't have any information on who his parents were or where he came from. He could have relatives who have been searching for him all this time. I want him to know if he has any of those connections or other family that I can't give him."

My phone chimes just then and I groan when I see the message. "Not again!"

"Did Scabby propose marriage?" she asks.

I ignore the crack. "This stupid lawyer keeps contacting me for information about Helena. I keep telling the dope that I don't know anything about where she is or what she's doing, but he won't listen. For all I know, he isn't a lawyer at all. He's probably another sucker she rolled and he wants his money back."

"I wouldn't be surprised," Quinn remarks.

I burst out laughing as I get near the bottom of the email. "Listen to this! This is priceless! This goon thinks Helena has been contacting me in secret and I've been holding out on him. Phew! What a shithead! Oh, no!"

Quinn spins around when she hears my tone change. "What now?"

"Maybe you wouldn't be doing Kai any favors by finding his family. My grandfather died last year and I'm supposed to inherit his money, except that I have to be married to get it."

"You are married, sweetie," Quinn reminds me.

"No, I mean, I have to be married for real with kids and all that. The lawyer in charge of my grandfather's estate just emailed to find out how close I am....and don't even get me started on my mother. She's been working overtime to find me a wife."

"Uh......sweetie....you already have a wife."

"Don't you think I know that? I've told them a million times, but they don't listen.... kinda like your family." I freeze and my eyes snap over to her. "Oh, my God! Why didn't I think of this before?"

She turns back to her computer. "Maybe because you were too busy planning how to take over the world from that downtown skyscraper of yours."

"No, seriously, Quinn." I hop off the couch and race over to her desk. "I just had a brainwave."

"Uh-oh. Not a good sign."

"Just listen. You could pose as my wife.... or wife-to-be."

She bursts out laughing. "Stop it. I could not. Your mother and your whole family already know we're just friends."

"That's exactly why it's such a brilliant idea."

"You are so modest," she sneers.

"Listen. Your mother and my mother and both our families have been on our asses for years to hook up and become a real couple. You could act like we were together and then I could get the money and no one would be any the wiser."

"But.... your grandfather's will states that you have to be married. You have to have kids and all that. We would actually have to BE married for that to work and we can't get married because you're still married to Helena."

"It would all be an act. You already have Kai so they would see me becoming a family man with responsibilities and everything. No one would ever know that we were really just friends."

"Why do you care so much about this money anyway?" she asks. "It isn't like you need it."

"I don't need it and I don't care about it, but it would be nice if I could just get everyone off my case about remarrying. Come on. Your family would get off your case, too."

"I don't know about this. It sounds like a terrible idea."

I fall on one knee by her desk and grab her hand. "Quinn Brown, would you make me the happiest man alive by becoming my wife?"

She laughs, yanks her hand away, and pushes me off. "Get away from me! Quit screwing around. We aren't getting married. Neither of us is ever getting married again. You're the one who keeps insisting that I stay a member of the Singles' Club forever and ever."

I go back to the couch and crash on the cushions again. "I went to your sister's wedding. Come to a family dinner at my parents' house next Saturday. Make them think we're getting married. It doesn't have to be for real. We can just string them along so they don't nag me all the time."

She turns around in her seat to stare at me. "You're serious! You really want to do this!"

"Yeah, why not? My mother loves you. Hell, my whole family loves you. What could possibly go wrong?"

She guffaws and turns back to her computer. "Don't ask that. Please. Never ask that."

"Come on, Quinn," I tell her. "You owe me at least one family dinner."

"Fine," she grumbles. "I'll just have to get a babysitter for Kai. Maybe I can ask Harper to do it. She loves him."

"No, bring him with you," I tell her. "It will be a hoot."

"Hoot?" she repeats extra slowly. "What will be a hoot?"

"Making my family uncomfortable when they realize I'm planning to marry a single mother. Bring him with you. We can get a few laughs when he causes chaos in the hallowed halls of the Aldrich Estates."

She shakes her head and turns away. "It won't be a hoot. It will be a catastrophe."

"Come on!" I tell her. "He'll love it. He's never seen my parents' house."

"No, he hasn't and I'd like to keep it that way."

I can see her putting up more resistance, but I'm so stuck on this idea that I don't want to let it go. "I'm calling in a favor. I went to your sister's wedding so you have to do it."

"Fine," she mutters. "I'll do it."

"You're the best!" I hop up and rush back over there to kiss her on the cheek. "This is going to be great!"

"A great mistake," she grumbles.

"Well, it won't cost you anything and you'll get a good meal out of it one way or the other."

She doesn't answer, but I can see the wheels turning in her head while she works on her computer. Neither of us wants to get involved with anyone, much less get married, not even on paper.

I won't be marrying Quinn because, as she constantly reminds me, I'm still married to Helena. In a way, this is the perfect solution to my problem. I can convince my family that I'm marrying someone without actually doing it. Quinn will never ask me to make this a real marriage because she doesn't want one.

This dinner is going to be the turning point for me. I'll never have to listen to anyone trying to set me up ever again.

Chapter 5: Quinn

Jayden gets out of his car, comes around to my side, and opens my door for me to get out. I'm wearing the same dress I wore to Karina's wedding and he's wearing the same tux except, this time, he's wearing a tie and a Rolex watch that looks like it cost more than my whole apartment building.

"Why are you opening Mom's door for her?" Kai asks when he gets out of the back seat. "You always do that."

"A gentleman always opens a lady's door for her," Jayden tells him and I blush and laugh nervously. I shouldn't be blushing about him opening doors for me. We're here to play an act, not to go on a date, but it sure is starting to feel that way.

Kai snorts. "Mom isn't a lady and you definitely aren't a gentleman."

Jayden turns around with not a trace of a smile. He actually looks dangerous. "Tell me to my face that your mom isn't a lady. Go on. Say it. I dare you."

Kai picks up on the change in tone right away. His smile evaporates and he wilts. "Okay. Sorry."

"You should be. Your mom is the nicest lady I've ever met. You should try treating her like a gentleman a little more often."

This is my cue to intervene. "So how exactly do you want to do this? Do you want to swap saliva in front of the lawyer?"

Now it's Jayden's turn to blush. "I don't think that will be strictly necessary."

"But advisable?" I'm getting too much of a thrill watching him squirm.

"What's swapping saliva?" Kai asks.

"Nothing you need to worry about," Jayden replies. "Come on, Quinn."

He extends his elbow to me and I take his arm the way I did at the wedding, but the stakes are so much higher here than at Karina's wedding. I actually have to act like Jayden and I are getting married. How the hell am I supposed to do that?

I don't have time to think about it. We're already walking up the long, sweeping driveway to the Aldrich Estates. This place is more like a massive castle than a house.

Most people know Jayden grew up in a wealthy family. Not many people realize just how wealthy the Aldrichs are. I'm the only person I know who has seen this place and still has Jayden putting his feet on the coffee table in my apartment.

This is the first time Kai has ever seen Jayden's parents' house and he reacts in the usual way. His eyes fall out of his sockets. He gasps and his eyes dart around trying to see everything at once. "Whoa! This place is huge!"

"Don't get lost," Jayden tells him over his shoulder. "You could be wandering around for days before the gardeners found you. Stay with me and your mom until you learn your way around."

Kai can't stop staring at the grounds disappearing into the trees, the fountains, the towering granite walls, the long twenty-car garage, the roof with the chopper pad sticking out past the gable, and the grand arches over the giant front entrance.

"Did you really grow up here, Jayden?" Kai whispers.

"Something like that," Jayden mutters. "Some would say I never grew up at all, but what do they know?"

Butlers in tuxedos bow to Jayden at the top of the granite front steps. "Welcome home, Sir," a wrinkled old man murmurs.

"Thank you, Merrick. You know Quinn Brown and this is her son Kai. They'll be joining us for dinner tonight."

The old guy bows to me. "It's a pleasure to see you again, Ms. Brown. If there's anything you need, please don't hesitate to let me and the staff know."

"Thank you, Merrick," I reply. "It's lovely to be back."

He glances at Kai, but Kai hides behind me and Jayden where Merrick can't see him. The old man shoots me a grin and his eyes twinkle. He purses his lips, but he doesn't try too hard not to smile. He doesn't greet Kai and the three of us keep going.

Two more tuxedoed butlers open the giant front doors for us and we glide into the foyer that rises all the way to a glass arched ceiling showing the evening sky above. The foyer leads to an enclosed courtyard full of trees buried in patches of soil surrounded by the floor stones.

The bubble of conversation leads us to the right where we enter a colossal hall adjacent to the grand dining room. Harper would be so jealous if I told her I was having dinner here. Aldrich Estates makes Karina's wedding look shabby and quaint.

Everyone wears evening wear and floats back and forth between walls hung with tapestries, oil paintings, and the Aldrich coat of arms. Statues stand in alcoves along the walls and potted trees arch over the room.

More butlers move through the crowd serving champagne and hors d'oeuvres to the guests. "Welp," Jayden breathes, "here we are again. I can never decide if I'm happy to come back here or not."

"How do you want to handle this?" I whisper back. "Are you gonna make a grand announcement about us being engaged to be married?"

"I don't know. I guess we'll just wing it."

"Please tell me you have some plan," I croak.

"Plan—me? I don't make plans. You know that."

I snort, but I make sure to do it silently. This guy runs a multimillion-dollar company. He can plan down to the tiniest detail when he wants to.

A woman's laugh draws our attention to the far side of the room and Jayden escorts me over there. Kai huddles close behind us turning in all directions to see everything, but he stays glued to my side every step of the way. He doesn't want to go anywhere.

Jayden stops next to a group gathered by a magnificent Steinway piano in the farthest corner of the room. An older lady with her grey hair piled on top of her head throws up her hands and exclaims, "Darling! You came! I'm *so* pleased! I missed you *so* much! My God, when are you going to cut your hair?"

She rushes Jayden, throws her arms around him, and kisses him on the cheek. She holds him at arm's length and beams at him. He smiles back at her in genuine delight and the other people in the group watch them together. "I missed you, too, Mama. It's good to see you."

Jayden's sisters Eva and Pauline smile, too, and Jayden leaves his mother to go over and hug them, too.

Jayden's mother turns to me, throws up her hands again, and cries out again. "Darling! Look at you! You're positively glowing! It seems like ages since I've seen you! How have you been? It's so delightful of you to come! You haven't been here in years! You should have come sooner! We would have loved to have you!"

"Thank you, Mrs. Aldrich. Thank you for having me. It's wonderful to be back here. It's so good to see you all again."

Eva and Pauline come over to greet me, too, and then I turn to Kai. "This is my son, Kai." I have to push him to get him to step out in front of me where everyone can see him and everyone beams at him.

"My God!" Mrs. Aldrich gushes. "Look how big he is! The last time I saw him, he wasn't much bigger than a football. It was such a tragedy how your husband died so young, darling. We were all heartbroken for you—but look what a magnificent job you've done raising this young man!" She grabs Kai's hand and shakes it hard. "It's a delight to meet you, my boy! Truly, a delight! Do you know your mother spent her weekends running around this house and the grounds and climbing trees and hiding under the furniture?" She bursts out laughing. "She practically lived here when she and Jayden were your age."

Kai's eyes pop all over again. "She did?" He looks back and forth between me and Mrs. Aldrich. "She never told me that."

"Sure, I did," I reply. "I told you that Jayden and I grew up together."

"You never told me you did it *here*." He starts looking around again. I can see I'm going to have some explaining to do when we get home and no one is around to interrupt.

Jayden comes back over to me, picks up my hand, and slips it under his arm again. "We have some news for you, Mama. Quinn and I are engaged to be married."

Her jaw drops and she gapes at him for a second before she screams out loud. "Oh, my God! You aren't serious! Are you serious? Congratulations, my dear!" She grabs me and crushes me in a hug.

Then it's all on with everyone in the room coming over to congratulate me and Jayden. Kai gets lost in the scuffle, but as soon as the mayhem dwindles enough for me to look around me, I see him across the room eating a finger sandwich, drinking sparkling grape juice out of a champagne flute, and talking to Merrick.

Kai looks like he's enjoying himself. I can just imagine the stories Merrick is telling Kai about when Jayden and I were kids.

I set off to cross the room to check on him when another mob of guests cut in front of me. They all want to shake my hand, hug me, and kiss me on the cheek while they congratulate me on the good news.

Each greeting and hug makes me more uncomfortable. Posing as Jayden's fiancé is turning into something a lot bigger than I realized.

I've known his family for decades. They've known me since I was a kid and Jayden and I have always been best friends. It isn't like he just showed up with some stranger off the street and told them he was marrying her.

We've had to repeat literally thousands of times that nothing was going on between us. Now we're reversing all that and his family reacts so much more than I ever anticipated.

Mrs. Aldrich keeps bursting into happy tears, hugging me, and telling me how this is the happiest day of her life. It will be the saddest day of her life when she finds out this is all an act to get her off Jayden's case about remarrying.

I'm not sure I can do that to her. I'm surprised Jayden can, but from the way he talks, she's been twisting his arm a lot harder than my mom has been twisting mine. Maybe he just can't take the pressure anymore and he already knows his family will accept me.

By the time I get over to Kai, Eva, her husband Stuart, Pauline, and her husband Reggie are all gathering around Kai. They talk his ear off about their kids, their houses, their pools, their horses, their properties outside of town, and all the wild adventures they want to take Kai on when he becomes a part of this family.

They fill his head full of helicopter skiing, waterskiing in Majorca, yachting around the world, parasailing in Australia, and rock-climbing in Peru.

He eats it all up and his enthusiasm encourages them to keep pouring out all these crazy ideas for things they want to do with him and places they want to take him once he makes friends with their kids who are his age.

I can't decide if I should stop this before it gets out of hand, but when I get there and see the wild glint of excitement in his eyes, I realize it's already too late. How can I disappoint him by telling him this isn't happening, either?

I open my mouth to say something when one of the butlers walks into the hall and rings a tinkling silver bell. It chimes over the hubbub and everyone turns away. Jayden takes my arm and escorts me and Kai into the grand dining room adjoining the hall.

I keep Kai close to me and make sure he sits in the chair next to mine. He doesn't make any embarrassing remarks when Jayden pulls out my chair for me and then pushes it in. We're supposed to be engaged. I'm only surprised he isn't acting more romantic around me to complete the performance.

I glance over at him while the butlers surround the table and start serving dinner. Jayden glances over at me at the same time and his eyes flash with some expression I've never seen before.

That isn't true, though. I have seen it before. He's just never used that expression with me. He usually looks that way when he looks at a woman he wants to hook up with. It's his seductive look—the look that usually makes a woman melt like putty in his hands.

That look makes my heart flip and a rush of fire shoots to my stomach. Why is he looking at me like that? He can't possibly want to hook up with me.... does he? Maybe he's just doing that to put on the act of being madly in love with me. How should I know?

That look grips me in an iron fist and he doesn't look away. He makes me meet his gaze so I can't look away. I feel myself starting to get turned on without meaning to. Is that what he's trying to do? Is he trying to send me a message about his real intentions?

That's impossible. He's the most dedicated member of the Singles' Club and he wouldn't hook up with me. He's the one who keeps saying that our friendship gives him his family fix without any obligations. He lives his need for family through me and Kai. He doesn't need anything else and he gets sex from his many hookups.

One of the servers comes between us and breaks my line of sight to Jayden. I face front and I make up my mind then and there not to look at him again for the rest of the evening. Why am I getting nervous about sitting next to my best friend? What the hell is happening to me?

The butler serves me and then Jayden. The instant the guy leaves, Jayden slides his hand across the table, covers mine, and squeezes. He doesn't just give it a quick press and withdraw.

He keeps his hand there and doesn't take it away. He keeps holding my hand until Mrs. Aldrich rises from her chair at the head of the table.

She raises her champagne flute. "This is a great day for the Aldrich family. I'm so pleased to announce the engagement of my son Jayden to his childhood friend Quinn Brown. Today will mark the beginning of a new era when our family will grow and thrive in ways we can only imagine today. Congratulations, my dears!"

The whole table chimes in with people calling, "Congratulations!" and "Here, here!" and a bunch of other stuff I don't hear over the noise. Everyone drinks to us, but I can't look at anyone.

How can I go through with this sham? How can I continue to hoodwink these people into thinking that Jayden and I have any kind of future together? I'm really starting to regret agreeing to this.

Everyone starts eating dinner and conversation restarts. No one notices anything wrong with me. I can't look at Jayden, but I want to leave. I want to take Kai and go home. I just want to go back to the way things were yesterday before all this craziness started when Jayden and I were just friends.

I somehow get through dinner without making a fool of myself. Jayden keeps pressing my hand and he bends toward me more than once to whisper in my ear.

"You're doing great," he whispers. "They're eating this up with a spoon."

His hot breath sears my ear and sends a cascade of sparks down my neck. Then he leans in extra close and kisses me right on the neck.

I shiver with electric tremors. Am I getting excited? He whispers to me twice more during dinner, and each time, he kisses me somewhere provocative just to seal the deal.

Each kiss sends another jolt through my whole being. Is he just acting or is he subtly trying to maneuver me into a relationship when he says he doesn't want one?

I can't figure it out, but his actions and constant touching are making my body react in crazy ways. I can't respond to him like this, but every move he makes seems carefully calculated to make me respond.

Is this how he acts around his conquests? Am I his next conquest? Is that what he's trying to tell me—that he wants me?

I try to shake that thought out of my head, but by the time we get up from the dinner table, I find myself trembling and fighting to breathe. I feel like I'm on a date. I feel like I really want him to take me home and conquer me in that way. Is this real? Are we still friends or did he just change all that?

He comes straight toward me after dinner and he stares down into my eyes with that powerful, intense look that makes me weak in the knees. He places my hand on his arm and that touch means so much more now.

I'm touching him through his sleeve. His body feels different standing next to me. He feels powerful and male and incredibly, magnetically, irresistibly attractive. No wonder women fall at his feet. How have I not noticed this about him before now?

I find myself easing closer to him so my body brushes his. My body wants to be near him and to feel how strong and male and sexually charged he is. He radiates impossible sexual energy that sets my every nerve on fire.

Is he doing this on purpose? Is he exerting his magic on me to make me want him? Is he even aware of the effect he has on me? I can't tell.

Kai doesn't notice anything. He's so delighted by all the Aldrich relatives making such a fuss over him that I'm not even sure he understood why everyone was congratulating him. How am I supposed to explain to my eight-year-old son that I'm not really marrying Jayden....am I?

Jayden steers me back into the hall where everyone mills around talking, sipping their drinks, and lounging on couches that the house staff brought in while we were eating dinner.

Jayden heads for one of the couches. "We can sit down over there. We can relax now and entertain anyone who wants to come over and congratulate us."

He laughs at his own joke, but I can't. I need to go home and lock myself in my room until I figure out what's happening to me.

What if I develop a secret attraction for Jayden? How can I keep being friends with him if I secretly want to do it with him? I'll become like Harper. I'll fantasize and pine for him praying for the day he suddenly wakes up and realizes that I exist.

I'm not sure sitting next to him on the couch is such a great idea. Is he going to kiss me and hold my hand there, too? Is he going to do something more?

All at once, he turns aside. "Oh, look! There's Farley Russo. He's the lawyer dealing with my grandfather's estate. He's the one who's been after me to get married. Come on. I'll introduce you and break the news."

I almost say something to try to back out of it, but Farley sees us first and his expression changes instantly. He's obviously already heard the news and he strides over to us spreading both arms to hug Jayden.

"Congratulations, son!" He claps Jayden in a huge hug. "This is great! I thought you'd never do it." He turns to me and holds out his hand. "Delighted, Ma'am! Truly delighted. You're a brave woman taking on this livewire!"

He laughs and Jayden joins in. I don't know what to say, especially when Farley lifts my hand to his mouth and kisses my knuckles.

Jayden distracts him by bumping Farley's shoulder. "So....what are we going to do about finalizing the divorce with Helena? How can we get this thing off the ground once and for all?"

"It's all settled," Farley tells him. "I've been investigating her for more than two years trying to find her for that reason alone. She really disappeared and didn't leave any trace, but just two days ago, I finally found her."

"So where is she?" Jayden asks.

"She's dead. She collapsed drunk in some gutter outside a bar in Seattle and died of hypothermia. You're a free man. You can remarry whenever you want."

He claps Jayden hard on the shoulder, but Jayden doesn't seem to feel it. He stares at Farley in stunned shock....and then Jayden's piercing eyes swivel over to me.

Chapter 6: Jayden

I get out of my car and spot Quinn and Kai across the playground at the park. Kai is climbing on the jungle gym and doesn't see me. Quinn has her back to me while she talks to some other mother.

I reach back into my car and lay on the horn extra loud. They turn around and Kai waves from the top of the jungle gym. I wave back and Quinn bursts into a huge grin and waves, too.

My heart lifts that I'm back here with them. Hanging out with them always makes me happy.

Quinn separates from the other mother and starts walking over to my car. Kai jumps down to the ground and races past her rushing me.

Quinn's beaming grin drains away and her face goes chalk white when I open the passenger door and Harper gets out. Harper waves to Quinn and Kai, too, but Quinn doesn't move. She stops dead in her tracks and doesn't come a step closer.

Kai doesn't notice anything. He charges me, collides into my side, grabs my arm, and starts towing me toward the jungle gym. "Come on, Jayden! They added some really hard routes to the climbing wall! You have to try it! Come on!"

"I'll be there in a minute, buddy," I tell him and turn back to shut the passenger door.

Harper puts her arms around my waist, kisses the side of my neck, and I become painfully aware of Quinn glaring at us. She's seen me making out with girls a million times, so why is this different?

Harper even slips her hand under my shirt as we make our way across the park toward where Quinn stands. Kai takes off back to the jungle gym. Now nothing remains but to walk over to Quinn with Harper hanging off me.

I stop in front of Quinn. Harper stops, too, since she's glued to my side. "Hi," I say.

Quinn's eyes slice over to Harper, but Quinn doesn't say anything. Have I ever brought a girl to the park when she and Kai were here? I can't remember. Is that why she's acting weird about Harper being here?

"I've been meaning to talk to you about Saturday," I begin again. Saturday was the night we went to have dinner at my parents' house, but she doesn't show any sign that I'm dropping a hint about that.

Just then, Kai calls out from the very top of the jungle gym. "Jayden—up here!" He waves to me again and I have to unwind my arm from Harper to wave back.

Quinn takes the opportunity to turn her back on me and goes back to watching her son scramble all over the equipment. A bunch of other rowdy boys are up there horsing around with him. He doesn't need his mother watching so this is just an excuse for her to ignore me and Harper.

I'm starting to understand why when Harper steps in front of me and presses her forehead to mine. "I better get out of here," she breathes and then she starts kissing me with her mouth wide open and plenty of tongue. "I'll see you later....Your place?"

"Sure," I reply as well as I can between her tongue slithering down my throat.

She rakes her fingernails down my back and darts her hands under my shirt again. She strokes my chest while we kiss and threads her fingers through my hair when she steps back.

She bites her lower lip and then runs her tongue over her teeth as she backs away. She points at me. "See you later."

I raise my hand. I want her to leave so I can find out what's wrong with Quinn. Why is she mad at me for hooking up with a girl?

It can't be because Harper is her friend. I've hooked up with Quinn's friends before and she never had a problem with it. She's seen me making out with girls way more than this.

I wave to Harper one more time before she walks out of the park. I turn back to find Quinn glaring at me in absolutely undisguised disgust. She curls her lip at me. That is definitely a first. "What?" I ask.

"Do you actually HAVE to?" she growls. "Do you actually HAVE to do it with her of all people?"

"Why? What's wrong with her?"

"Nothing is wrong with *her*. You're the douchebag here, not her."

"Since when am I a douchebag? She's a consenting adult. She practically threw herself at me and I don't see her running in the other direction to get away from me. I was at my apartment minding my own business and she barged in and practically ripped my clothes off."

Quinn groans, rolls her eyes, and spins away. "Spare me the gory details, okay?"

"What's wrong with you?" I follow her when she walks away from me. "What's the big deal? It isn't like you don't know what I've been doing with these women. What's your problem?"

"Could you not do it with her? What's the matter? Have you worked your way through every other single woman in town?"

I gape at her, stunned. Did she just say those words to me? Since when did she get so hostile about my love life?

She turns away again and heads off into the park, but at least she does it slowly enough for me to keep up with her. Her body language tells me that she wants me to stay with her. She isn't trying to walk away from me for real.

I don't know what I'd do if she did walk away from me for real. I experience an overwhelming tide of relief and gratitude that she's still willing to talk to me. She wants to work this out. She's disturbed about something—something that affects our friendship. That's why she's telling me. She isn't dropping me like a hot rock.

What would I do if my player ways really bothered her? What would I do if me being a player meant she wouldn't be my friend anymore? Would I stop playing the field if it meant keeping her friendship?

I don't even have to ask. I would stop in a heartbeat if I thought playing around threatened our friendship. Should I tell her that? Should I tell her just how much power she has over me?

I ease up next to her. I want to hold her hand the way I did at dinner the other night, but my better judgment wins out. "What's going on?" I ask in an undertone. "What's bothering you?"

She throws up her hands, but she won't look at me. "It's just her. She's.... she's fragile."

"Really? She doesn't act fragile." I don't elaborate. Quinn knows Harper a lot better than I do. I don't really know Harper at all.

"She gets involved with guys, gets her feelings all tangled up with them, and then, when it doesn't work out, she gets her heart broken. She's done this a dozen times. It's always the same."

"So what are you saying? You said you don't want me to mess around with her, but it's a little late for that now. Do you want me to dump her?"

"No!" She whips around fast and confronts me before she realizes and turns sideways so she doesn't look at me, but she doesn't walk.

"Don't dump her. I mean, I know you're going to dump her anyway, but don't do it because I want you to. That will just hurt her even more."

"What am I supposed to do? It isn't like I have any feelings for her. I already explained that to her and you said you explained it to her, too. You said you told her what I'm made of."

"I did," Quinn mutters. "I tried to warn her about you. I told her to stay away from you."

I snort and realize too late how bad it sounds. "She didn't. She definitely didn't."

"I knew she wouldn't, but she lied to herself that she would be the one to change you. She told herself that you had to stop being a player someday so why not stop with her? I told her it wouldn't work and I knew you wouldn't be interested in her. I told her straight out that you wouldn't like the fact that she wanted you for your money."

I freeze and my blood runs cold at those words. Quinn. She knows me so well. She's probably the only person alive who could actually say those words to me.

She's known me since we were kids. She played under the furniture in my house. She climbed trees in the grounds and skinned her knees on the driveway.

She has never, NEVER once even mentioned my money. She never cared about me having money. She never asked me for money or acted at all interested in dating me because of my money.

That's one of the things I most admire about her. She worked her ass off for years to support her son alone. She worked her fingers to the bone to give him a decent life.

She could have asked me for help. I could have given her a year's rent out of my wallet, but she never asked. I could have made sure she never wanted for anything for the rest of her life. I could have paid for Kai to go to the most expensive private school in town.

I would have done all that in a flat second if she only asked, but she never did. She wanted to do it herself. She wanted to wear that effort as a badge of honor. She wanted to say that she raised her son on her own and I love her to death for that.

She did all that while still being my friend. She never once let money come between us. I could hug her for that, but that would only drive a wedge between us right now.

Only she could say to my face that she noticed all these tramps throwing themselves at me for my money. Only she could actually mention something like that in conversation.

I don't know what to say, so she turns away. "Just forget it. It doesn't matter. It's over and done with like you said. It's just that I'll be the one she comes crying to about how you broke her heart."

"How can I break her heart when we aren't even involved?"

"I know," she mutters. "You don't have to explain it to me."

"Why didn't you tell me not to mess with her?" I ask. "Why didn't you tell me you didn't want me to go there with her?"

She spins around fast and her eyes blaze. "You would....You wouldn't have....?"

"Of course not. I never would have gone near her if I thought you wanted me to stay away from her. I would have slammed the door in her face. You made it seem like she knew what she was getting into and didn't care."

"You seriously...wouldn't have......?"

"Of course not! We're friends. If you told me not to, I wouldn't touch her with a ten-foot barge pole. Our friendship is way too important to me."

She keeps staring at me like I just landed from another planet. How can she not know how important she is to me?

"So what do you want me to do about it now?" I ask. "You don't want me to dump her, but it isn't like it can come to anything. She's boring and…. shallow. She doesn't even try to hide how interested she is in my money. It's really kinda scary how obvious she is about it."

"I know. I know it can't come to anything. Just let it run its natural course."

"Okay. If you say so."

She turns away and doesn't look at me as we continue to stroll through the park.

"So… are we cool?" I ask.

"Yeah," she mutters. "We're cool."

"Thanks."

She shrugs. This is obviously still bothering her…or something is.

"Did you have a good time on Saturday?"

"Of course. You know I love your family."

"That's what I wanted to ask you about. Now that Helena is dead, I'll be looking to marry someone."

She snorts and doesn't try to hide how bad it sounds. "Good luck."

"I could marry you," I suggest.

She spins around so fast her hair whips across her face. "You what?"

"Why not? It would work out for both of us and you and Kai went down so well on Saturday. My family knows you and you know them. It's the perfect solution to our problem."

"It isn't the perfect solution to anything because I don't have a problem. I don't want to get married and I don't have to marry anyone to inherit my grandfather's money. It's the perfect solution for you so you don't have to actually get involved with anyone."

I try to shrug it off. "It's just an idea."

"Well, forget it. Having dinner with your family so they get off your case is one thing. We aren't getting married for real. No way."

"Okay. Forget I said it."

"I can't forget it because you already said it. You can't seriously expect us to get married—for real. You're on drugs."

I force a laugh. "I must be if I suggested something that you think is so ridiculous."

She turns away and starts walking again, but she definitely wants me to stay with her. She doesn't walk so much as meander one slow step at a time. I do the same thing and we move side by side through the park.

It's nice and peaceful walking next to her. I didn't think anything could ever develop between us. I didn't want it to and she obviously doesn't want it to. That's all right with me. We'll just keep being friends, but I can't help but wonder.

What if? She sure is nice and I already love her like a.....well, I might have loved her like a sister a few days ago, but things changed on Saturday night.

Kissing her, holding her hand, looking over and seeing her by my side....What if? What if we could be a real couple like that? What if I could take her as my wife to have dinner at my parents' house? What if she and I lived together to raise Kai together?

We spend all our free time together as it is. I'm in and out of their apartment every other day and I'm the man in Kai's life. I don't have to wonder about that, but we've always had a brotherly, uncle-nephew relationship. I've never been a father figure to him. We're too close for that.

Would I become a father figure to him if Quinn and I got married? Why am I even thinking that when she obviously doesn't want to? She acts like marrying me is the worst thing that could possibly happen to her.

It's never going to happen, but it sure is nice to think about.

Chapter 7: Quinn

I jump out of my desk chair when I hear loud footsteps coming toward my apartment. It sounds like someone is running fast and hard.

I barely get a chance to turn around before the door blasts off its hinges and Harper barrels in. I catch one glimpse of her face streaked with tears before she throws herself on the couch sobbing her eyes out.

"He dumped me! Jayden dumped me—the cocksucker! How could he do this to me? How could he just use me and throw me away? Doesn't he have any feelings? Doesn't he care about me at all? This is a disaster!"

I sink back into my chair watching her from my desk. This is so typical. I saw this coming a mile away and she's gone through the same thing with every other guy she goes out with.

I can't even say she's dated them because she doesn't date. She hooks up with players and this is how it ends. I can't even say I told her so even though I did.

I can't blame Jayden for this. He never leads women on, and if he told the truth about Harper showing up at his apartment and nearly ripping his clothes off, she couldn't reasonably expect it to turn out any other way.

She knew his reputation. I told her and I'm sure she heard it from other women. There are plenty of women running around this town who will tell anyone who stands still for two seconds what a player and a user and an asshole Jayden Aldrich is.

Quite a few of them aren't above going back to his apartment when they feel like it. They're happy to use him back as long as they can keep complaining about him in public.

I've known Jayden for years and if there's one thing I've learned, it's that he doesn't delude these women about his intentions. He would never tell a woman he was interested when he isn't. He doesn't do that.

"Why does he have to be so callous about it?" she wails. "He doesn't even try to be nice about it. He just said he was bored and he never wanted anything more serious than a fling. I mean, who says that? Who treats people like that? What is wrong with him?"

I don't say anything. There's no answer for this. I grab a box of tissues and go sit next to her on the couch. She'll get over this in a week or two. Then she'll set her eye on some other dude and go through the whole process again.

She'll become one of the many women who has slept with Jayden Aldrich, but she won't sneak back to his apartment in the dead of night to enjoy herself with him. She'll forget he even exists.

She blows her nose loudly. "Don't ever go out with that guy, Quinn," she tells me. "He's bad news."

"Okay. I won't."

She was the one telling me after the wedding that I should get involved with Jayden. She was the one telling me that he and I should be a real couple instead of just pretending.

She throws her tissue on the coffee table and grunts in disgust. "What a prick!"

"When did it happen?" I ask.

"Just this morning. I stayed over at his place last night and I thought...." Her face screws up in a twisted mass of agony. "I thought it was beautiful! I really thought we had something....and then this morning......he just.....ended it!"

She bursts into even louder sobs. She grabs another tissue, presses it to her nose and mouth, and howls into it.

I scoot over next to her and put my arm around her. Of course she would mistake great sex for connection. Considering the way Jayden was looking at me at that dinner, I can see now how he could bewitch a woman into thinking he felt something when he didn't.

He obviously didn't feel anything for me when he looked at me like that. He's just gone straight back to being my best friend since that night. He doesn't act like he wants anything.....except for that ridiculous suggestion that we make this whole marriage of convenience thing a real....whatever it is he's suggesting.

He blew it off by saying it was just an idea, but he really meant it. He wouldn't have said it if he didn't mean it. Why in God's name would we get married?

He probably looked at Harper like that while he was looking at her, but as soon as they weren't in bed together, he went back to seeing her for what she really is. She's boring. She's shallow. She doesn't even try to hide that she's only interested in his money. What guy in his right mind would want a woman like that?

I don't say any of that out loud, though. She's already upset enough. Saying that would only make it worse.

I could never marry him, not even knowing that his money would take care of me and Kai for the rest of our lives. I would never have to worry about money ever again, but I couldn't do that.

Besides, we're just friends. I wouldn't marry a guy I didn't have strong feelings for and I don't feel that way about him. He doesn't feel that way about me, either, so that answers that question.

Harper brings me back to reality by blowing her nose again and turning to me. "I really appreciate you being there for me. I really need a friend to talk to right now."

"Don't worry about it. I'm sorry it didn't work out."

"You're the best, Quinn." She hugs me. "You deserve a decent guy. I'm sorry I said you should go out with him. I wouldn't want that to happen to you."

I have to smile at her. "Thanks. I wasn't planning to."

"You should get with someone, though," she goes on. "You shouldn't live alone like this."

I snort. "I'm doing okay on my own. I don't want to bring a man into Kai's life. Our lives are complicated enough as it is."

"No, really. You haven't dated anyone since Max died. You should find someone. You're still young and you're drop-dead gorgeous. Everyone says so."

I roll my eyes. "Don't start. You sound like my mom. I'm not going to start dating anyone. I have enough to do working full time and raising my son by myself."

She opens her mouth to answer when we hear the elevator ding down the hall. She left the apartment door open when she came in, and before either of us can move, Jayden walks in carrying a six pack.

He yells out his usual, "I brought beer!" before he sees me and Harper sitting on the couch.

His expression goes cold when he sees Harper's bloodshot eyes and tears staining her cheeks. His mouth pinches in a tight line and he throws his car keys on the counter way too loudly.

She glares back at him and then hurls her tissue on the coffee table in what would be a challenging gesture if the tissue made any noise at all. She humphs, swings to her feet, and tosses her hair back. She snaps, "I'll see you later, Quinn," and stomps out of the apartment.

I collapse back on the cushions and cover my face with my hands. "Spectacular. Just goddamn fantastic."

"Let me guess," he replies. "I'm a jerk and a prick and an asshole and a cocksucker and a douchebag."

He grabs a beer, comes over to the couch, and throws himself down next to me. I can't stay there sitting so close to him or I might start feeling the way I did at dinner.

I get to my feet, but I don't want to sit anywhere else with him in my apartment. I pace around not doing much of anything and go to the kitchen to shut the apartment door. "She's all heartbroken like I knew she would be," I tell him.

"I only told her the truth. I told her the very first night she came over. It isn't like I lied to her or anything."

"You don't have to tell me. I know all about it."

"Are you still mad at me over this?"

"Why would I be mad at you?" I call over my shoulder. "You didn't do anything."

"Why are you acting mad, then?" I pick up the laundry basket and he follows me down the hall to the laundry room. "Why are you walking away from me? What the hell happened with you? You've been pissed off at me since....well, I don't know when it happened, but something sure did."

I spin around to confront him. "You want to know what happened? You asked me to marry you. What did you think was going to happen?"

He bursts out laughing. "I did? When?"

"When you asked me to have dinner with your family. You went down on one knee and took my hand and asked me to make you the happiest man alive by marrying you."

"I was just joking around! You know that! I was making a joke about putting on an act for my family. Come on! You know I wasn't serious."

"Oh, yes, you were," I counter. "Don't lie about it. You might have been joking then, but you weren't joking when you kissed me at dinner and you weren't joking at the park when you said we should get married for real. Just admit it. You want us to get married—for real."

He shrugs. "Okay. So what if I do? You know I love you. You're the only woman I can stand to be in the same room with for more than a few days. I don't seem to be able to keep away from you, and now that Helena is dead, you're the only woman I can think of that I want to marry."

"You just said a few days ago that you never wanted to remarry at all! You've been saying for years that you wanted to stay single for the rest of your life! You don't want to get married! You're the biggest player on the block! You just burned through another piece of ass THIS MORNING! How can you even think about marrying anyone? Forget about it. It's stupid. It's brainless."

The faintest hint of a smirk creeps across his lips, but he manages to bite it back when he hears me going off on him. "Maybe I keep burning through all these pieces of ass because they aren't you."

"Oh, give me a break, Jayden! You don't want to get married and you sure as hell don't want to marry me. I can't for the life of me figure out why you keep bringing it up."

I start to turn away toward the washing machine when, lightning quick, he grabs my arm, spins me back around to face him, and kisses me right on the mouth. He does it so fast and I'm so surprised that I freeze in place.

I can't move and now I'm staring into those eyes at close range. Those brilliant eyes blaze at me from just beyond my nose and they catch me in the same overpowering undertow. How is he doing this to me?

The same rush of exhilaration and desire grips me that I felt at dinner. I want him. I want him bad.

I haven't felt this for any man—not since Max. I didn't even feel this way about Max. Max never electrified my every nerve this way. I loved Max with a much warmer, more comfortable, mundane love.

This is lightyears different. This simmers like lava buried in the heart of a volcano just waiting for the right trigger that will make it erupt off the Richter scale. This will explode my whole world apart if I let it out.

I can't feel this. I break away and shove the laundry basket between me and Jayden. I have to keep something between us before that feeling makes me fly completely out of control.

I use the laundry basket to push him away, out of the laundry room, down the hall, and toward the kitchen. I can push him out of the apartment there. "Get out of here, Jayden," I tell him. "Just go home. Leave me alone."

He resists, but he doesn't stop me from pushing him out of my apartment. He walks backward fast to keep up with me.

"No, Quinn! Don't push me away! Talk to me! We can work this out! Just tell me why! I love you! I love you more than any woman I've ever met in my life, even more than Helena. Why can't we at least talk about it?"

"Forget it!" I fire back. "You're a player! You're the biggest player in town! Why in God's name would I want to marry you?"

"I changed! I want to change. I don't want to play around anymore! I want you! I love you! Please, Quinn! Just tell me why. Why won't you marry me? I love you!"

"You love me as a friend. You only want to marry me so you can inherit your grandfather's money. You aren't in love with me, not really. This is just a marriage of convenience for you and I don't want that."

"It could work for both of us. I could take care of you and Kai. Come on. You don't have to work so hard all the time. What do you say?"

"Is that what you think? You actually think I would marry you for your money? How can you insult me like that?"

I give him one last show into the kitchen, and for some reason, I stop there. I don't go any further.

"I know you wouldn't!" he counters. "That's what I love about you. You never asked me to. That's exactly why I want to. I love you and you love me. Isn't that enough?"

He lunges for me and grabs my arm again to stop me from walking away, but at least he doesn't kiss me again. We don't seem to be yelling at each other anymore, either.

I study him for a second. I can think of a lot of reasons not to. "No," I finally say.

"Why?" he counters. "Just tell me why?"

"Besides all the reasons I just mentioned? Because I don't want Kai growing up ultra-rich and pampered and spoiled rotten. I worked hard to raise my boy right and I won't sell him for a stack of cash so he can grow up living at Aldrich Estates. I want him to grow up normally and to have a normal life."

His jaw drops as if he really didn't expect me to say that. "Is that it? You don't want Kai to grow up rich? Is that the only reason?"

I hesitate a second time. "If you're serious about stopping all this fooling around that you do, then yeah, that's the only reason—apart from the fact that we don't love each other. I mean, we aren't *in love* with each other."

"What if I move in here with you and Kai? What if we keep living the same lifestyle with no change except that we're married? I already spend all my time here anyway."

I gape at him in horror. He's serious. He really means it.

He must be serious if he's suggesting that. He wouldn't have us living at Aldrich Estates. He would live in my dumpy apartment and keep our lifestyle the same.

Before I can come up with an appropriate response, he takes a step toward me. He very slowly and deliberately pushes the laundry basket out of the way. He goes through every movement with such precision and intensity that I can't move.

He eases one excruciating inch after another closer to where I stand. His power grips me in an unbreakable hold.

"Marry me, Quinn," he whispers under his breath. "I love you. We might not be in love now, but we could be. I could be. I want to be. I want everything with you. I want only you. I don't want things to go back to the way they were before. I love you...."

He sweeps his hand behind my back, and in a split second, he pulls me against his body. His muscular frame ignites this deep, passionate well of insatiable desire, and just like that, it breaks through the top of the mountain and explodes my life to smithereens.

His lips crush against mine and rock me in a hurricane of sensation. His body goes stiff and taut and his crotch bulges against my leg before he shoves it between my thighs.

His mouth sucks the air from my lungs and I gasp in ragged agony as his lips consume me. His tongue sizzles with mind-blowing energy and his hands creep a little lower toward my ass.

Before I know what's happening, his hands take possession of me. Everything he does ruptures the barrier holding back my deepest desires. My body aches for him and my pulse throbs between my legs when he drives into me.

I sob in desperation. I need him. I need him bad. I need everything he's describing and I need it now.

He seizes my ass and smashes my sensitive tissues into the pulsating mass of masculine power between his legs. He rotates me on it and his eyes demand that I show him all my deepest needs when I moan in ravenous hunger.

He takes a step and slams me into the fridge, but he smothers me in such rabid, scorching kisses that I can't stop what's about to happen. He crawls his hands lower to my thighs, grabs me by both knees, and lifts me up to his waist.

He pulls my legs around his hips and plows in hard. He drills me with a steady rhythm that leaves no doubt where this is going. I can't stop it and I don't want to. I need him to own me and conquer me and take me all the way. I can't live without it.

He rips off my mouth and a tortured hissing groan escapes him when he spreads my legs apart. That breaking wave of delirious passion makes me move with him whether I want to or not. Our bodies join in a steady beating journey to one destination. There's no stopping it.

He holds me by one leg and his other hand slides along my cheek to clench in my hair. His eyes won't release me as he searches my deepest soul for the part of my heart that will love him the way he wants me to.

I can't resist the power of his will. He started it at dinner with his eyes and hands and lips. Now he completes the spell and my surrender is complete. He knows it when he looks into my eyes. He knows I'm already his.

His lips shiver when he inhales each raspy breath. His jaw clenches and his tongue barely touches the inside of his teeth. His mouth looks so incredibly fucking hot, but I can't kiss him. I have to undulate against him watching my destiny get closer and closer.

I gasp and pant trying to scream out all the painful need burning me up right now. He sneaks his fingertips farther up my thigh toward the seam of my jeans. He'll be able to touch me there and then......

At that moment, the elevator dings out in the corridor. Footsteps approach across the carpet, but these are much softer. It isn't an adult. It's Kai coming home from school.

Jayden drops my legs instantly and steps back. My feet hit the floor and I bolt down the hall back to the laundry room. I can't let Kai catch me with Jayden in the kitchen. I don't trust myself not to give something away.

I stand there panting hard and listen to Kai and Jayden talking out in the kitchen. Kai doesn't think anything of Jayden being in our apartment. Jayden twists off the cap of one of his beer bottles. His voice and Kai's voice drift away toward the living room.

Jayden can handle this a lot better than I can. What am I supposed to do with all these feelings welling up in me right now?

"Mom!" Kai calls out. "Where are you?"

"I'm down here!" I struggle to keep my voice steady.

I take the laundry basket and head up the hall toward the living room. I walk in and smile at Kai like I was just up the hall doing the laundry. Nothing to see here.

Chapter 8: Jayden

I pace up and down in my office with my phone pressed to my ear. "I heard he disrespected your friend at her sister's wedding," Jason Emery tells me. "I just want you to know I took care of it. He doesn't work for our brokerage anymore."

"I never asked for that," I reply. "I gave him a warning and he took it. If he straightened himself out, then that's good enough for me."

"I know," he replies. "This wasn't about that. He acted up at the office. His behavior has been getting more and more unacceptable for a while. We had to do something about it."

"Okay. I understand. Thank you for telling me. I appreciate it."

"I just want you to know I took care of it," he repeats. "I wouldn't want something like this to interfere with our business relationship."

"It doesn't. I'm fine with it."

"Is your friend all right?" he asks. "He didn't....do anything to her?"

"She's fine. He didn't do anything. He was just being an ass in public."

He laughs. "Of course. Well, now he can go be an ass somewhere else. It won't happen again."

"Thank you. I appreciate it."

He hangs up and I toss my phone on my desk. I turn back to the big windows looking down on the town from my skyscraper office window.

The instant I stop thinking about business, my mind switches back to Quinn. That conversation didn't make me think of her. I've been thinking about her ever since yesterday. I can't stop thinking about her.

My God, what have I been doing with my life? Why have I been burning through all these pieces of ass as she calls them? Why have I been screwing around with a bunch of women I don't care about and I don't even like when I could have a woman like her?

Why haven't I been looking for a woman I could really love—someone I would want to dedicate my life to? Why haven't I been looking for that one woman who would make me forget that every other woman on the planet exists?

I haven't been looking for her because she's been right there in front of my face the whole time. I've been slouching around in her apartment and hugging her and kissing her on the head and joking around with her and eating dinner with her and Kai....and I never knew.

I really am a jackass. I'm every bit the douchebag she says I am. Of course she doesn't want to marry me. Why should she when I've ignored her for so long?

I value her friendship, but only because it never challenged me to be anything more. I never let myself go there and feel anything for her—not like this. I'm sure feeling it now, though. I can't stop feeling it.

I can remember the soft compression of her lips when I kissed her. I can feel her hot breath burning my face and the drunken, raving madness in her eyes. I can feel every quiver of suppressed lust pulsing through her tight, hot body. Holy fuck, can I feel all those things!

None of those things comes close to this feeling in my heart—the unstoppable need to love her. I have to love her. I have to give my whole life to her and Kai. The thought of living with them makes me unspeakably, stupidly happy. It makes me feel complete. Those words sound so trite and cliché, but so, so true.

I'm half a man without her—without both of them. I'm a cripple without them.

I have to marry her. No wonder my grandfather put it in his will that I had to be married with children to inherit his money. I'm a child without that. I'm a toddler who has been bumbling around the world playing with toys. I've never been a man and I won't be until I take on this responsibility and carry this burden.

What a prick I've been to let Quinn carry it all alone. I never should have let her do it herself. I should have insisted. I should have taken that burden off her shoulders. That's what a man would have done.

What man would stand by and let a woman he loves—even a woman he loves as a friend—go through that torture without doing something? I'm blind. I'm insensitive to the point of cruelty. I don't deserve her.

I'll change all that. I'll marry her and make her happy. I'll relieve her worries. I won't let her suffer anymore. That's the bare minimum I can do with my life and my money. It makes my success worth it that I can dedicate it to something worthwhile for a change—something other than getting laid.

I go back to my desk and start cruising around the internet. I can think of a lot of things I could do with her and Kai. I can think of a lot of houses I'd like to see them living in and schools I'd like to see Kai going to and places I'd like to take them, but Quinn's warning keeps coming back to me.

She wants Kai to have a normal life. She wants him to grow up as a normal boy, not as the pampered rich. She doesn't want him living at Aldrich Estates or jetting around the world.

I am going to have to seriously restrain myself from pushing her to do more and be more. That isn't what I love about her. I don't want to change her and I don't want to change her lifestyle, not really.

Hanging out with her in her apartment and screwing around with Kai at the park is what I've always loved about them. I don't really want to change that and throwing money at them won't make any of us happier.

I can only do that by being different—by being the man they need me to be. I can do that.

I'm in the middle of that when my phone rings again. The screen says, *Edwina Aldrich.*

"Hi, Mama," I greet her. "Is everything all right?"

"Darling!" she exclaims. "Eva and Pauline and I have been talking all about the wedding. We want to get together with you and start making plans...."

"What wedding?" I ask.

"*Your* wedding, darling!" she exclaims. "Your wedding to Quinn, of course. We need to book the caterers and the band and the decorators and the dressmaker, which means we need to set a date. When can you and Quinn come back to the estate to discuss it? And you absolutely HAVE to bring that charming boy with you! He's delightful!"

My ears prick up. Set a date? Quinn hasn't even agreed to marry me yet.

She did a lot more than not agreed to marry me. She did a lot more than turn me down. She was horrified by the whole idea.

She wasn't horrified by the idea of doing it with me, though. She responded to me like I couldn't believe. I can still convince her to go through with this.

"I'll have to talk to her about that, Mama. She's pretty busy."

"Well, when can you talk to her? We need to start planning right away. A wedding this big doesn't just happen overnight, you know."

I can just imagine what Quinn will say when she finds out that my family is already planning a wedding this big. "I'm seeing her tonight, Mama. I'll ask her about it then."

"Let me know right away, darling. We're all in stitches about this. We couldn't be more pleased. I want you to know that. You two have been so close for so long. It couldn't happen to a nicer couple. I'm so pleased!"

I smile into the phone. Of course my family loves Quinn. Who doesn't? "Thank you, Mama. I'll tell her you said so and I'll get back to you as soon as I can about the meeting."

We hang up, but the conversation gives me all kinds of ideas. I keep seeing her in that dress at the dining table at Aldrich Estates. She looked angelic then. She looked like a queen and she fit right in.

She's always so down-to-earth, so humble and straightforward. She isn't part of all that high-blown society built on money. She just wants to be normal. That's what made her my friend in the first place. She made me believe that I could be normal, too. I didn't have to be a snob with a stick shoved up my ass.

Her skin felt immaculately soft when I whispered in her ear and kissed her on the neck. She lit my whole being on fire, not because she was a woman that I wanted to touch and caress and conquer. I can get that anywhere.

No, it was the way she made me feel that really blew my mind. I wanted her to live in that world with me. I wanted her to be my wife, the woman on my arm, the woman at my side, the woman who leans on me and needs me and makes me a man. I need that from her.

I can't concentrate on work so I leave the office and wander around town, but I always wind up wandering back to her place. Her apartment attracts me with a hypnotic pull. I don't want to be anywhere but with her. It's always been like this. Why would I want to be anywhere else?

It's already past eight o'clock at night. Kai will be in bed. I don't usually come over this late, though it isn't unheard of. She won't be able to mistake the subtext if I do come over now, but maybe that's for the best.

I knock on the door and my heart skips a beat when I hear her footsteps coming nearer. I'm going to see her in a fraction of a second. Can I handle that?

The door opens and she stands before me as beautiful as ever—and as defensive as she was when I left yesterday. She holds the door to block me from entering. Her eyes challenge me with an unmistakable, What-are-you-doing-here glare.

I can't even smile at her. I just want to stand here gazing at her until she closes the door in my face. I don't say anything. She can see in my eyes that I want her. I don't even try to hide it from her. I want her to know how I feel about her. I want her to know how much I crave her and love her and need her.

She compresses her lips, looks away once, and straightens up without softening her stance at all. This is definitely the first time she's ever made me stand outside the door. It's even the first time I've ever knocked on her door. I always just went right in before.

"What can I do for you?" she finally asks in a short, annoyed tone.

"Can't we at least talk about this, Quinn? Are we just going to throw our friendship away over this?"

"You're the one throwing our friendship away. You're the one saying you don't want things to go back to the way they were before."

"I can't go back to the way they were before. I can't stop myself from wanting to marry you."

She snorts and rolls her eyes. "If you can't go back, then what is there to talk about?"

"Can't we at least discuss it? Can't we sit down and have a civil conversation about whether there's a way to come to a mutually agreeable decision about how we're going to handle this?"

"How can there be a mutually agreeable decision? You want to get married and I don't. There's no middle ground on that."

"Why isn't there? We haven't even discussed if there could be."

"What middle ground could there be?" she counters. "Either we get married or we don't. We're either married or we aren't. There is no in-between."

"Can't we at least sit down and talk about it?" I ask again. "We're supposed to be friends."

"That's what I thought, but apparently I was wrong about that."

Those words wring my heart. "We are friends, Quinn, and if none of this comes to anything and we stay nothing but friends for the rest of forever, I'll be happy with that. I never want to lose your friendship—not ever. If you don't want to be friends with me over this, I'll drop the whole subject."

"Drop it now," she snaps. "Drop it now and don't ever bring it up again. I already don't know if I can trust you not to make a move on me and mess everything up again."

"Okay. I'll drop it. Can I come in now?"

She sniffs at me and turns away. "Fine."

She walks away from the door and leaves a path for me to go inside, but I still take a second to decide to do it. I have to be careful here.

She's right, of course. The comfortable trust we used to share isn't there anymore. I ruined that by asking her to marry me. Can we ever get it back?

Chapter 9: Quinn

J ayden walks into my apartment much more carefully this time. He doesn't usually come over this late at night. I should be going to bed right now. I have to work tomorrow morning, but he's right. We need to figure this out.

I need to know now if we're going to be friends or not. I need to know if we're really going to get into some kind of relationship, though I can't imagine what that would look like. We've only ever been friends. I'm not sure I can think of him as anything else.

He sits down on the couch, but he doesn't slouch or put his feet on the coffee table like he usually does. He just sits there like he's at a job interview or something.

Seeing him like this twists my guts. Our friendship obviously means a lot to him, but I can see that his feelings have changed. What if he never lets this go? What if we stay friends and he keeps wanting me...forever? Can I live with that?

The thought of losing him hurts—a lot. I don't want to admit it to myself, but the thought of losing his friendship scares me in ways I've never been scared before.

He's stood by me for years. He's been the one person I could count on through the darkest, toughest, loneliest years of my life. I couldn't have survived without him. I wouldn't have been able to raise Kai without Jayden's constant company and support.

He could have given me money if I asked for it, but he gave me something a thousand times more valuable. He gave me himself. He gave me his attention, his comfort, and his conversation. He gave me a friend. I can't live without that. That's the truth. I would rather die than live without it.

I sit down on the armchair across the coffee table from him, but when I actually let myself feel how much I need him in my life, I wind up moving over to the couch. I sit down on the opposite end so there's no chance of us touching, but at least we're sitting on the same couch. The world hasn't ended yet.

He looks over at me and I can see in his eyes that he still wants me. He'll look at me like that from now on. Can I really deal with that?

He doesn't say anything. He just sits there staring at me. I should be the one to say something. If he doesn't, I have to.

"Well?" I finally blurt out. I hear myself snapping at him, but I don't know how else to start this off. "What middle ground do you say there is between us getting married and us not getting married?"

"I don't know," he replies. "Maybe just staying friends."

"Then we don't get married," I counter. "You're still going to sit there and wish we got married."

"Can you blame me? I want to get married. I can't just stop myself from wanting that."

"Then we aren't compromising, are we?"

"Can you compromise at all?" he asks. "Is there any way you can take a step toward the middle ground?"

"How—by getting married? That isn't compromising, either. That's capitulating."

"I'm not asking you to capitulate. I'm asking you to work with me to preserve our friendship."

I cock my head to one side and study him. "Are we friends? You aren't acting like a friend. You're acting like a man who wants to marry me. Even if you agree not to marry me, you'll just keep wanting that, won't you? We won't be friends anymore."

Those words stab me in the heart and tears spring to my eyes. I want to break down crying at the thought of us not being friends anymore. My mouth twists and I grimace in agony fighting back sobs. I have to turn away to stop him from seeing, but it's too late.

He crosses the couch in a fraction of a second and wraps his arms around me. "I'm so sorry, Quinn!" he breathes into my hair and his voice breaks. "I'm so sorry! I never wanted anything but to be friends with you! This is all my fault! Please forgive me! I can't lose you! I can't lose our friendship! You're the most important person in my life. I can't live without you. Please forgive me! I need you so much! Please.... just let us be friends again. Please."

I can't stand those words and I break down crying in his arms. I need him so badly. I can't live without his friendship, either.

I feel him holding me and kissing my hair and the side of my face. None of that is any different from what we've always done. It doesn't feel any different. We're just friends. He's comforting me as a friend and it feels good. It's a relief to know we still have this.

I lean back and straighten up, but I can't stop the tears from streaming down my cheeks. Nothing I've ever endured hurts worse than the thought of losing what we have.

He keeps petting my cheeks, wiping the tears off my face, straightening my hair, and kissing me on the forehead. He rubs my arms and back and then he pulls forward the box of tissues I left here after Harper's visit.

"You okay?" he asks when I calm down.

I nod down at my lap.

"Just forget about us getting married," he murmurs. "Nothing is worth this. Hurting you isn't worth it."

"Thanks," I mutter. I feel like I just got hit by a truck.

He leans back on the cushions and relaxes the way he used to. Is he really going to just drop this? I glance up at him to find him looking at me with his old friendly smile. He looks happy. Maybe there's hope after all.

"Are you okay with this?" I ask.

He shrugs. "I'm happy being friends with you. If this is what it takes, I'll do it. I'll do whatever it takes to make it work for you, even if it means dropping it." He glances around the apartment. "This place has always been more my home than anywhere else. You and Kai have always been my family—more than anyone else. I don't want to lose that. I don't care how it happens as long as it stays the way it is."

"You won't go back to wanting it?"

"I'll always want it." He threads his fingers through my hair and kisses me on the cheek one more time. "But I can live without it for your sake. You're too important to me. I just thought.... well, it could have been awesome, but I guess it just wasn't meant to be. I'll just have to tell my mother and sisters that we won't be meeting them to talk about the dress and the cake and the caterers and the band and the flowers and the decorations and setting the date and all that."

I freeze staring at him and my jaw drops. "They're already planning the wedding?"

"Sure. They love you. They're over the moon about us."

"And you.... you went along with this?" I stammer. "You let them think we would....like that......?"

"Of course I did. We're supposed to be getting married. What did you think was going to happen?"

"But I thought....I thought you would......I thought you would keep it low-key—like maybe we would go off to the county courthouse and just get it done on the side. I thought you would......"

I break off searching his eyes and face for some answers. Why did I think the Aldrich family would let us get away with that?

Of course Mrs. Aldrich would want to go over the top with a huge estate wedding. Jayden is her only son. She and her daughters would pull out all the stops.

What surprises me is that Jayden would go along with it. He's been so anti-relationships for so many years. If he really went along with planning this wedding, he must really want this to be real. It isn't a marriage of convenience for him if it ever was.

I find myself looking into his eyes at close range. He sits so close to me on the couch. I can feel his body inches away from me. His lips and eyes and skin breathes with all the powerful energy I senses in him yesterday—the energy that came to life when we started kissing.

He just said that this apartment is his only home and Kai and I are his real family. He isn't saying anything I don't already know. He's said it before and I know it's true, but he always meant it as a friend before.

Marrying him would just make it official. We would still be a family and, if he was serious yesterday, this apartment would still be our home.

Now I realize with a lurch that he means something so much more than that—something so much deeper. He wants us to be more than family as friends. He wants us to go all the way. He wants us to fall in love and dedicate our lives to each other in *that* way—not as friends.

What's the difference? I find it harder and harder to tell where the line is anymore. Is there a line at all or do I only see one there because

I'm so resistant to accepting his proposal? What would make that line disappear besides me just saying yes?

He smiles down at me exactly the way he always did when we were friends. We're still friends, so why do I see him as more? Am I looking at him the way he looked at me right before he kissed me? Am I looking at him like I want him?

I want to kiss him, and for some reason I can never figure out, without discussing it or any change in either of our positions, we both move in at the same time. We kiss and keep on kissing to the ends of the Earth.

I can't get enough of him. Kissing him makes me feel how much I want him, but this is different from yesterday. I want more than just to release this buried passion I've been keeping hidden since Max's death.

I want to feel what he's showing me. I want to cross that line. I just don't know how. He's my home and my family the same way I am to him. What if I could cross that line and erase the difference between loving him as a friend and loving him as a man? Is that even possible?

My desire for him erupts the way it did yesterday, but now it gets all tangled up with so many other feelings. I want to love him. I just don't know how to stop being friends with him.

I seem to be doing a pretty good job when he leans over and his hands appear on my ribs right behind my breasts. I arch into his touch as my body takes command of my movements.

I ache for him and he doesn't disappoint. His tongue coils in magical circles in my mouth and he tastes incredible. His muscles tenses under his jacket and then he starts tugging it off. His broad shoulders, chest, and arms electrify me when I touch him through his shirt.

His fingertips creep a little closer to my spine and then his warm, strong palms slide forward under my arms and close over my breasts.

I gasp in a sudden wave of pleasure. He's touching me and I'm touching him. He lies down half on top of me and tips me against the arm of the couch as he moves closer to me.

I don't want to stop this. I want to go all the way and see where it leads. I raise one knee and he lies down between my legs. His weight lights me on fire and my body undulates with rising energy.

His hot breath drifts into my nostrils and his eyes leave me nowhere to hide. I see in those bottomless pools that we're actually going to do this. We're going to do it right now....and then what?

Without warning, he grabs me, sweeps me off the couch, and sits me up straddling his lap. His hands run up and down my spine and his fingers close on the back of my neck to steer me into his kiss.

That commanding hold makes me melt into his grasp. I sink into him savoring the delicious feeling of him holding me. He makes me feel safe and protected. He accepts all that I am. I never have to worry about anything with him, and in that moment, I feel the depth of love between us. It's been there all along. He's my closest friend. He's the most important person in my life apart from Kai.

I see the same truth in his eyes when he eases back and opens his eyes to look at me. His hands and lips and body tell me that he doesn't want that to end. He wants us to keep loving each other even though we're sharing something we've never shared before.

He slides both hands down my sides, breaks off my mouth, and nibbles down my neck to my chest. He mouths my breasts through my shirt, but he doesn't do anything else until I peel my shirt off myself.

He groans in bliss when he drags his scorching lips over my skin. His hands explore every part of me, but he keeps his touch soft and gentle while his mouth crawls lower toward my bra.

I have to take my bra off. I have to feel his mouth all over me and I need my skin touching his skin.

I throw my bra away and moan in ecstasy when he starts kissing and sucking my breasts. I can't stop running my fingers through his hair and hugging his head against my chest while I drag his shirt up his back.

He raises his head just long enough to pull his shirt off and then he dives in to attack my breasts in greedy mouthfuls. His hands massage every inch of my body while his mouth drives me to the stars.

I have to hold back my ragged moans of rising passion. I don't want Kai to hear us. Him coming out here to see what's going on would be my worst nightmare.

Jayden must be thinking the same thing because he stops manhandling me and glances up the stairs. We can't stay out here, but I don't want to stop.

"Let's go to your room," he tells me.

I stand up and pick up my shirt and bra. I don't feel even slightly self-conscious that I'm walking around topless in front of Jayden. It feels natural somehow.

He picks up his shirt and jacket. He seems much taller and much broader in the chest and shoulders now that I'm seeing him with his shirt off. Have I ever seen him with his shirt off before?

I can't remember if I ever have, but I definitely don't remember him being this big or this intimidating. His long hair makes him look rugged and wild.

He places his hand on my lower back for a split second to steer me out of the room. That touch makes me quiver with excitement. I don't have to wonder what we're going to do when we get to my room.

We go upstairs and I shut the bedroom door. Jayden throws his shirt and jacket on the chair and kicks off his shoes before he comes toward me.

His eyes don't leave me in any doubt what he plans to do. He looks at me with the same smoldering intensity I've been seeing for the last week. I can't stop seeing that look all the time now and my insides squirm as desire takes hold of me.

He kisses me and I collapse into the effortless tide pulling me toward him. Is it possible that this was always meant to be? Why am I fighting this?

His hands and body tell me so many secrets I never let myself see before. My hands explore the indentations of his chiseled torso and I feel him twitch and jolt at every touch. His breath catches and he burrows across my cheek, behind my ear, and down my neck.

I fight to breathe as he reaches my chest again. No one can hear me moan in here. No one can see how desperately I need this. I need him. He's the only one who can break down this armor holding me back.

He pulls me toward the bed and we both topple onto our sides kissing faster and harder and deeper. Our tongues twine together in a seamless sea of boiling lava. It saturates my mind. All I can think is how much I want him right now.

We both crawl up the bed and then, for no reason whatsoever, we both break apart. We go into a flurry of activity tearing down the covers, diving inside, and then stripping off our pants as fast as we can.

He starts laughing and I can't stop myself from joining in. This whole situation is ridiculous in such a heartfelt, comforting way. We're about to do it in my bed for the first time. Nervous giggles take hold of me and I dive into bed, pull the covers over my head, and hide in the darkness from the rising agitation at what's about to happen.

He hunkers down next to me still laughing. He crawls under the covers and pulls them over his head so no light comes through. He raises his voice to an artificially high-pitched, sing-song quaver that sounds like a little old lady. "Where are yooooooouuuuuuu?"

We both explode in laughter, and in that dark place, we come together in a hot, satin rush with nothing holding our bodies apart.

He feels incredibly good. His body trembles with the tension of holding back deep desire and his legs wind around mine before he pulls one of my knees against his side. He works himself between my legs so he can't fail to feel how wet I am when our bodies touch.

His hard shaft grazes my leg and then he's between my legs exactly where I want him to be. His body meets mine and we lock together in such a magical spell of bliss and luscious passion that I don't even try to hide it.

I moan into his mouth as he moves with me. He overwhelms me with ecstasy and my body explodes in escalating bliss.

He rolls on top of me and the covers fall away. His eyes blaze down at me from above and his hair surrounds my face as we kiss. His chest and shoulders swell to an impossible size when he props his arms on either side of my head. He glares down at me in between diving in to snatch kisses from my mouth.

He rears all the way up and pumps into me with strong, powerful thrusts that launch me into full, screaming delight, but I still have to keep quiet. I can't stand him looking at me like that and I feel myself reaching the peak of climax. If I keep going like this, I really will scream.

I bury my face in his chest and neck and muffle my cries on his skin. He groans louder and thrusts deeper with me in that position. I wrap my arms around his ribs and hang on as he propels me higher than the highest stars.

I scream into his neck as my body dissolves around his rock-hard shaft and I hear him whispering in a tortured, breathless rush. "Oh, yes! Fuck, yes! Fuck! God, yes! God damn!"

His agonized voice throws a switch in my brain and I collapse against him sobbing in matchless rapture, but he doesn't stop except to kiss the side of my head. He follows my rhythm and keeps me spinning on continuous spikes of pleasure. He won't let me come down.

All at once, he lowers his head and presses his mouth against my ear. He husks in a tormented panting gasp building up to his own release. That sound exhilarates me beyond anything I've experienced yet and I scream into his neck to match his pace. I have to stay with him. I have to reach that place with him so I can share it with him.

Without warning, he straightens up, nudges my head down, and clamps his lips on mine in a ravenous kiss. His eyes snap wide open and he gasps striking deep and straight and true.

He convulses all over and gasps again and again with every trembling spasm gripping his midsection. His eyes drill me to impossible depths as his body pulsates inside me. His muscles trigger an answering response in me and I freeze staring up at him in the throes of crushing ecstasy, but I can't look away. I have to see him owning me and conquering me like this. I have to see it all before we both collapse in a breathless heap on the pillows.

Chapter 10: Jayden

I wake up and squint into the sunshine before I remember where I am. I roll onto my back and look out the window. I'm in Quinn's bedroom—in her bed.

I sink back on the pillow and throw my arm over my eyes as all the memories of last night cascade through my mind. She is so unbelievably sweet and perfect. I can't get enough of her and now I'm here, in her bedroom, in her bed.

It's morning and I hear her talking to Kai downstairs in the kitchen. I check the bedside alarm clock. It's seven-thirty. She'll be getting Kai ready for school and then she has to walk him downstairs to the bus stop.

After that, she needs to start work on her home computer. I should get out of here, but I can't do that with Kai around.

I relax in bed enjoying all the memories of last night. This is the first time I've ever done it in a woman's bedroom. I always take women to my place. I don't know why. It just always works out that way.

It won't work out that way anymore. Last night sealed the deal. We'll get married and I'll move in here. Then we'll do it in here all the time. That will be wonderful. I can't wait to explore every secret corner of who she is.

I wish she was here right now for me to kiss and I start getting hard again just thinking about it, but this morning isn't the time. It will be like this a lot when we're married. She'll have to take care of Kai and I won't be able to just tear her clothes off whenever I want to with him around.

That's okay. Minding my manners around him will only make me want her more. It will make the times we share together sweeter and more delicious. I never thought I would ever think that not doing it with a woman could mean more than doing it with her, but now I know it's true.

This is how I know she's the one. This is right because not doing it with her means more than doing it with her. Even waiting in this bed makes me happy because she's right there in the next room. She's doing her job by taking care of her son and I'm supporting her by letting her do that. I'm supporting her by getting out of her apartment so she can concentrate on work.

That's what she needs from me. She needs me to understand and to make allowances for her needs. I love her for that. I love being that for her. I want to be the only man alive that does that for her. It's such an honor that I get to be that man for her.

The front door opens and shuts and silence descends over the apartment. She'll be back soon and then she'll want me to leave so she can work.

I take the opportunity to get up and start putting my clothes on. I'll go home and take a shower before I start my day. I don't need to do it here.

I stick my feet into my shoes, pick up my jacket, and go out to the living room. I'm ready to go, but I want to kiss her before I leave. I want to let her know how much this means to me.

I sit down at the kitchen counter and scroll through emails on my phone while I wait for her to come back. I put my phone in my pocket when I hear her footsteps approaching down the hall outside.

She walks in and looks surprised to see me out of bed. "Are you okay?" she asks me.

"I'm wonderful." I pull her toward me. "Last night was spectacular. Thank you."

She lets me kiss her, but she isn't bubbling over with enthusiasm. Is that because she isn't enthusiastic or am I just too used to women gushing at me about how wonderful last night was? I can't tell.

She waits until I finish kissing her and then she starts to turn away. She really is about to walk away without saying anything.

I catch her at the last minute. "Hold it. Are you okay? What's wrong? Do you regret what we did last night?"

She barely glances at me before she looks away. "I don't know how I feel about it."

I open my mouth to say something and stop. What am I supposed to say? It isn't like I can make her enjoy it after the fact. "Did you at least have a good time?"

"Sure," she says way too shortly. "You know I did."

"Does that mean......?" I don't know what it means.

"I'm okay," she mumbles. "I just need to figure out how I feel about it."

I go through several rapid thought processes just to make sure I didn't do anything last night that might have put her off. She seemed to enjoy it at the time and then we both fell asleep in each other's arms.

"I meant what I said," I tell her. "If you aren't okay with this, we can just quit. None of this is worth risking our friendship."

"I think we're way past that now, don't you?" She finally levels me with a direct stare when she says this and I gulp at the look in her eyes. She's right. Are we even friends anymore?

I can't stand thinking that. I draw her between my knees, cup her cheeks in both hands, and kiss her. She kisses me back much more deeply than she did a moment ago. She doesn't just tolerate it.

She kisses me deeply and passionately, but a hint of sadness creeps into her lips. Is she kissing me goodbye? She better not be.

A beep on her phone interrupts us. She doesn't try to move away when she pulls it out of her pocket. "I gotta start work. I'll talk to you later tonight if you want to......"

She breaks off staring at her phone. She goes stiff and tense. She doesn't see me right there in front of her.

She taps the screen and her eyes glaze over. All at once, she jolts away from me. "No! No no no! No! It can't be!"

She takes off pacing around the kitchen and staring at her phone.

"What's wrong?" I ask.

She shakes her head still staring at her phone. "I don't believe it! It can't be! It just can't!"

"What's up?" I stand up and walk over to her. "Is something wrong?"

She spins around fast, plants her hand on my chest, and shoves me away hard. "Don't come near me!"

"What's wrong with you?" I gasp. I don't want to know.

She crushes her phone in a white-knuckle grip and glances back and forth between me and the phone with huge, terrified eyes. Her lips tremble and she holds out the phone as if me looking it will somehow answer all my questions.

"What's wrong, sweetie?" I croak. "What happened?"

"It's......the...." She gulps hard, shuts her eyes, and shudders all over before she summons the courage to speak. "The....private investigat or.....the one I hired to find Kai's parents.....He found Kai's mother."

"Who is she?" I ask.

"She's.... she's dead." Her petrified eyes dart to her phone and then lock on me with unimaginable power. "She died of hypothermia in an alley behind a bar in Seattle."

I don't understand at first what she's saying. I frown and then the puzzle pieces click into place. Seattle. Hypothermia. Where have I heard those words before?

Helena died of hypothermia in an alley outside a bar in Seattle.

Quinn buckles over her phone and her whole body wilts before my eyes. Her voice trembles with barely suppressed sobs and I can see her shaking from here.

"The Medical Examiner determined that she'd just given birth a few days before. The PI canvased the whole city and found out that she gave birth in a women's shelter. She registered anonymously and wouldn't tell anyone her name. She abandoned the baby at the shelter and disappeared. None of the shelter workers knew what happened to her and they put the baby into foster care."

I barely hear her with the blood rushing in my ears and I definitely don't see her. Kai. He's mine. Helena must have run away because she got pregnant. That explains why she didn't say anything to me before she vanished out of my life with no warning.

Kai. That boy I've been spending almost every day with for year s.....he's my.....son. His mother was my wife. She got pregnant before she left me, which means......he's mine.

"Say something," she croaks. "Just....say *something*."

I snap alert and burst out laughing. "This is great! This is perfect! This is the best thing that's ever happened to me." I walk toward her and spread my arms to hug her.

I bend down to kiss her on the cheek, but she shoves me away with all her might and springs back with a shriek. "What are you doing?! This is a disaster! Do you realize what this means?"

"It means Kai is my son. I can't believe it!" I can't stop laughing. The happiness bubbles out of me uncontrollably. "Don't you see? We can get married and be a real family now. It's perfect! Nothing will stop us."

"Are you insane?!" she roars. "We are NOT getting married! Do you honestly think you're just going to move into my house and start being a father to my son just because we did it once? Are you out of your head? Forget it!"

"I am a father to your son. I'm his father. You don't have to marry me, but you can't keep him away from me. I'm going to get custody and we'll start seeing about...."

"Custody!!" she shrieks. "Are you stupid? You can't get custody! I'm his mother! Who the hell do you think has been raising him all these years?"

"You can't push me out of his life." I try to stay calm, but she's so irate that I find myself getting defensive. "You adopted him, but Helena stole him from me which means that the adoption wasn't valid. I never gave him up. I would never do that. If you don't at least let me see him and be a father to him...."

"You aren't his father!" she bellows. "You're a stranger!"

Those words set off something in me that won't go back to sleep now that it's rearing its ugly head. "I am his father and you can't stop me from getting him back."

Her jaw drops and she gapes at me in horror. She blinks like she doesn't even recognize me. "Get.... him......back......"

"That's right. He's my son and I'll do whatever I have to do to make sure I'm the father he deserves."

I don't give her a chance to answer before I turn on my heel and stalk out of the apartment. I leave her standing there with her mouth open.

I have a son. Friendship means nothing compared to this. If she tries to stop me from getting Kai back, I'll fight her to the death to make sure he knows I'm his father. I've never been more certain of anything.

Chapter 11: Quinn

"It's time to go, sweetie!" I yell up the stairs. "Get your backpack and come on. We have to catch the bus."

"I'm coming, Mom!" Kai calls from his room.

I put the last dishes in the dishwasher and wipe down the kitchen counter before I go over to my desk. I'm in the middle of laying out a few things for work when someone knocks on my door.

I answer it and a young Asian guy hands me a sealed manila envelope the instant I open the door. "You've been served. Thanks. Have a great day."

He walks off and leaves me stunned. Served? What does that mean?

I take the envelope inside and examine it just as Kai comes down the stairs. "I'm ready, Mom. What's that?"

"I'm not sure. Go put your shoes on."

He sits down by the front door while I get the scissors out of the kitchen drawer. I slit the envelope open and pull out a pile of papers.

The floor falls out from under my world when I read the headline. *Motion to Vacate.* Jayden is challenging the validity of Kai's adoption exactly the way he said he would.

I can't read the papers. I can't even look at them. I turn my head aside and press my hand to my mouth trying to hold back this gut-turning anguish.

My boy. I can't lose Kai. He's my whole world. How could Jayden do this to me? How could my own best friend stab me in the back and twist the knife like this?

"Mom?" Kai asks behind my back. "Are we going? You said I'd miss the bus."

I can't look at him. He has no idea. How could I ever tell him that......? Jayden isn't his father. Jayden hasn't been a father to Kai. They've been friends or maybe brothers. Jayden has never been a father and he never will be.

"Mom?" Kai asks again. "What's wrong?"

"Nothing, sweetie. Let's go." I try to shake it off, but I can't stop my voice from quavering.

He swivels in front of me and looks up at me with crystal green eyes—green eyes exactly like Jayden's. Helena had blue eyes and Kai's eyes are lighter than Jayden's, but now I see the resemblance in ways I never noticed before. It's all too horribly true. Jayden is Kai's father.

A tear streaks down my cheek, and once it starts, I can't stop it. I can't let anyone take my son away. I might as well be dead without Kai.

He doesn't ask again what's wrong. How stupid it is to expect him to believe that nothing's wrong when he can see plain as day that it is. Everything is wrong. Nothing can ever be right ever again.

I clamp my eyes shut trying to block this whole nightmare out of my awareness, but as soon as I open them again, I have no choice but to look at Kai's face. I'll never stop seeing Jayden every time I look at my son—Jayden's son.

I gulp down despair and try to look anywhere but at Kai. I catch sight of the clock on the microwave. We're too late for Kai to catch the school bus, but that doesn't seem to matter anymore. Nothing is as important as this, and if Jayden wins and takes Kai away from me, Kai needs to know what's going on.

His eyes question me and his face pinches with worry. He's scared. Maybe he should be, but I can't leave him in any doubt about why.

I take his hand and lead him to the living room. "Come over here and sit down, sweetie. I need to talk to you."

"Is something wrong, Mom?" he croaks. "Is someone dead?"

"No one's dead. Sit down." I sit him on the couch, sit down next to him, and take his hand. "You know I love you, right? You know I would do anything for you. You know that, don't you?"

"Yeah? What's going on, Mom?"

I take a deep breath. I have to do this. "You know the story about how Jayden's wife left him without warning and never came back?"

"Yeah?"

"It turns out that she was pregnant. She had a baby in Seattle and then she died a couple of days later. No one knew who the baby belonged to and they put the baby into foster care. I.... I adopted you in Portland. She was your mother.... which means that Jayden is your father."

He blinks at me in the same stunned blank that Jayden stared at me when I told him. Kai and Jayden really are copies of each other. They're father and son.

All at once, Kai bursts out laughing. I'm having a serious déjà vu from my conversation with Jayden. "Seriously?" Kai exclaims. "He's my dad? This is great! He's the best! I can't wait to see him! Wait until he finds out!"

"He already knows, sweetheart."

"This is gonna be great! Just wait until we get to the park.... or the climbing gym! This is the best!" He starts laughing again. He's so happy.

"There's just one problem, darling. He wants to go to court to say that the adoption wasn't valid. He wants to cancel the adoption so he can get you back."

My son's face drains of all color and I start sobbing when he gapes up at me in horror. "You mean....he would take me away from you?"

"I don't know, baby," I choke. "I don't know what's gonna happen, but I'm going to do everything I can to make sure you stay with me."

"But that means...." he begins, but I can't listen to this.

I fold him in my arms sobbing hard. I can't lose my son. I've already lost Jayden. I can't lose Kai, too.

Thinking that makes me cry even harder. My whole world is coming apart at the seams. This is even worse than when Max died. My life would be over without Kai. It feels like it's already over.

I finally push him back and wipe my face on my sleeve. "Anyway, we need to get you to school."

The scared look in his eyes makes me want to cry again, but I need to pull it together for his sake. "What's going to happen, Mom?"

"I don't know, sweetheart. I really don't, but the most important thing is that we get you to school. We'll try to keep things as normal as possible until we know for sure."

"But.... I already missed the bus."

I want to dissolve in tears again. What difference does it make if he misses school? This is way more important, but keeping him at home to dwell on this will only make him more agitated. I'm already agitated enough for both of us.

"I'll drive you to school, sweetie. Come on. Let's go."

I hold onto his hand and lead him out of the apartment. He keeps glancing at me on our way down the elevator and across the parking garage to my car. I do my best to smile at him, but all those unanswered questions still hang in the air. They won't go away.

We get in the car and I drive him to school. He still has ten minutes to get to class. I park in front of the school and turn to him. "Try not to dwell on this too much. Dwelling on it will only worry you and it's going to be a while before any of this gets resolved. Just try to have a good day and keep doing all the same things you usually do."

He opens his mouth like he wants to bombard me with questions about what's going to happen to him. I wish like anything I could answer those questions. I would do anything to take that worry away from him, but it's hard enough just carrying it myself when I don't know if someone is going to take my son from me.

He finally looks down at his hands and nods. "Okay. I'll try."

"I love you. I'll always love you and I'll never stop being your mom no matter what happens. Okay? Do you understand? No one can stop me from loving you. I'm so very proud of you. I'm going to do everything I can to make sure this works out the best for you. Okay? I promise you that I am."

He leans against me and puts his arms around me. "I love you, Mom."

I have to seriously fight back tears when he gets out of the car. I smile and wave to him, but the instant he walks into the school, I bury my face in my hands and collapse in tears. I can't take this. I can't face this. It hurts too bad.

I have to face it. I have to beat this. I have to find a way to stop Jayden from doing this to me and to Kai.

Jayden obviously doesn't care about what's best for Kai if he doesn't realize how much taking Kai away would hurt him. Jayden doesn't have any children. He doesn't know how much Kai needs me.

I know it, though. It's my job to make sure no one hurts my son like that. I drive back to the apartment, but I won't be getting any work done today. This is way more important.

I take all the court papers that Jayden served me with and I drive into town to see Jenny Warren, the same family court lawyer who handled Kai's adoption.

She hugs me when I go into her office. "Look who's here! How's the munchkin?"

"He's okay...." I try to smile and wind up tearing up instead.

Her mouth falls open in horror when she sees me crying. "What's wrong?"

I hand over the paperwork and she stares in horror at that, too. I slump in the chair by her desk and wait for her to finish reading everything.

"My God!" she breathes. "This is a nightmare!"

"Tell me about it," I growl. "Please tell me there's something you can do about this."

She doesn't look up. She stares at one page after another as she flips through Jayden's motion. When she finally raises her eyes to meet mine, I realize the worst. There's nothing we can do. Jayden is holding all the cards.

Jenny compresses her lips and rests her elbows on her desk while she decides how to break the bad news. "Jayden Aldrich is a friend of yours, isn't he?"

"He was before this happened."

She spreads her hands. "Then my suggestion is that you contact him and try to work something out with him. If he's a friend of yours, maybe he'll understand why you have to stay in Kai's life. Maybe he'll let you keep seeing Kai even though....."

She doesn't finish and now it's my turn to gape at her in sickening horror. "*Let* me see him? He'll *let* me see my own son?"

"It is his decision.....or it will be if he succeeds in this motion. The adoption will be nullified which means that all your parental rights will be nullified, too."

I can't listen to this. I want to run from the room, but she isn't telling me anything I didn't already start to suspect. Without the adoption, I have nothing.

My own words come back to haunt me. Without the adoption, I'm just a stranger in Kai's life. I'm a stranger who's been feeding him and putting him to bed and taking him to school and comforting him when he's sick for eight long years.

I'm the stranger that stayed up all night with him when he was a baby. I'm the stranger that worked eighty hours a week to pay the bills and buy his clothes and take him to the climbing gym on Saturday afternoons.

All of that will mean nothing if Jayden succeeds in nullifying the adoption. Jayden never has to let me see Kai ever again. I would have to beg Jayden on my knees to let me see my own son.

I hate him for that. I hate for doing this to me. How could I ever consider him my friend?

Chapter 12: Jayden

I pace around my office not getting any work done, but I don't care. Kai is my son! I can't believe it.

I can't wait to see him and talk to him. My mind won't stop spinning with all the things I want to do with him. I want to take him everywhere and show him everything. I want to spend every waking minute with him. I would have been spending every waking minute with him if I only knew he was mine.

I have eight years to make up for and I'm going to start right now. I call Stuart Ross, my sister Eva's husband. He's the Deputy Police Commissioner downtown.

"What's up?" he asks me when he answers the phone.

"Hey, man. You know that trip you said you were planning with Simon and Andrea—the horse trekking trip you mentioned—the one you invited to take Kai on?"

He hesitates. "Who's Kai?"

"Kai Brown—Quinn's son—the boy that came to dinner at the estate last weekend."

"Oh, right! Yeah, I remember. What about it?"

"I want to come with you....and I want to bring Kai."

"Okay," he replies. "That won't be a problem."

"Could you email me all the information? I want to start booking air travel and everything....and are you coming out to the estate any-time soon?"

"I wasn't planning on it," he replies. "Why do you ask?"

"I want to make a time when you and Eva are going to be there.... and bring Simon and Andrea. I want Kai to meet them."

"Great idea!" he exclaims. "How about.... what about this week-end?"

"Sounds good. We'll be there."

We hang up, but the conversation only makes me more agitated. I can't sit still thinking about introducing Kai to all his relatives. I want him to come to all our family functions and get to know everyone.

My mother is going to have a heart attack when she finds out. That's why she's been on my case for so long about remarrying. She wants me to have children.

This is even better than the fantasy about marrying Quinn. Kai is my son—my real son. I try to believe it even as I tell myself not to believe it in case it turns out to be a cruel trick of some kind.

I can't wait to see him, and when I leave the office on my lunch break, I wind up driving to his school. I sit out in the parking lot staring at the front entrance. I have to fight myself not to barge into his classroom and start talking to him right now.

I want to talk to him about everything. I want to know everything he's thinking at every minute of the day. I want to tell him all about my childhood and how I became successful. I want to make sure he does well for himself and what better way than to teach him how I did it?

I count down the hours until five o'clock, and when the bell rings, I get out of my car and approach the school gate to meet him.

He bursts into a massive grin when he sees me. His cheeks flush and I can't help but blush when I grin down at him. He's my boy. He looks just like me. Why didn't I see it before? I feel like I'm looking at a younger version of myself.

"Hi," I say in a shaky voice.

"Hey," he replies.

"Um.... did your mom tell you?" I ask.

He nods, but he won't stop grinning at me. He's as excited about this as I am.

"Are you okay?" I ask. "Are you okay with it?"

"You mean.... with you being my dad?"

Infectious laughter escapes me and I can't stop my cheeks from burning. "Yeah. That."

"Yeah," he replies. "I'm okay with that."

"You remember when Stuart mentioned going horse trekking with his kids next summer vacation? I was thinking we could go together. You could meet your cousins and get to know my family—I mean, you could get to know them better than you got to know them at dinner the other night. It would be better if you hung out with them somewhere not so formal. You and his kids could just run around being kids together."

He lights up as never before. "You mean it? For real?"

"Yeah. It will be a lot of fun."

His face falls and he glances sideways. "What about Mom? She says you're trying to take me away from her."

My stomach drops, not because of what he's saying. What else could vacating the adoption mean besides taking Kai away from Quinn?

It's the look of abject terror on his face that really turns my stomach. I could fool myself as long as it was just me talking to myself in my own head. I could trick myself into believing that being with his real family would be better for him than being the adopted son of a single mother.

I can't lie to myself when I see how distressed he is by the thought of leaving her. He isn't just distressed. He's petrified. She's all he's ever had. She's his mother in every way that counts. She's a hell of a lot more his mother than I am his father.

Some brainless, sadistic part of me might have been willing to do that to her, but I could never do that to him. He would never recover from that. Losing her would destroy him. He doesn't give a damn about me and my family compared to how he feels about her.

His eyes dart sideways and his expression does another about-face. He explodes into another beaming smile. "Mom!"

He rushes away from me, crosses the school driveway, and charges into his mother's arms. Quinn hugs him while she glares at me over the top of Kai's head. She narrows her eyes at me in an unmistakable look of murderous threat.

She keeps her arm around her son when she stalks across the driveway to confront me. "I don't appreciate you coming here unannounced."

"What's the big deal?" I ask. "You never had a problem with me hanging out with Kai before. Now shouldn't be any different."

"I might be willing to believe that if you weren't trying to take my son away from me. If you want to see him, I'd appreciate it if you let me know so it looks less like you're sneaking around behind my back."

"I would never take your son away from you, Quinn," I tell her. "That isn't what this is about."

"How am I supposed to believe that when you're trying to nullify all my parental rights by vacating the adoption? How could you do this to me, Jayden? You know what Kai means to me and no one knows better than you do how much raising him has cost me."

Her voice cracks and tears pour out of her already bloodshot eyes. Seeing her upset makes me feel even worse. My throat constricts. I want to put my arms around her and comfort her, but I'm the one who caused this.

I'm the one who made her cry like this and I'm the one who terrified Kai with his worst nightmare a few minutes ago. I did that.

"I don't want to take Kai away from you," I tell her. "Can't we come to some agreement so we both get what we want?"

"I don't see how. Come on, Kai." She steers him away.

"Wait, Quinn!" I call out. "Don't leave! At least talk to me about this."

"I can't. I can't even think about talking to you as long as I have this motion hanging over my head. Just leave me alone, Jayden. Leave both of us alone."

She walks off toward her car with her arm still around Kai's shoulders. He tries to twist around to look at me, but when he does, I see that he's just as scared and upset as she is.

I did that. I threatened him with the worst fate a child can suffer. I threatened to destroy the only home and family he's ever had.

There has to be a way to fix this. I just have to figure out what it is. I have to figure it out fast before everything I love vanishes out of my life forever.

Chapter 13: Quinn

I lean against the railing and wave to Kai high up on the climbing wall. He clambers over spherical obstacles, lunges for the next ledge, catches hold, and scrambles to the top.

He punches the flashing red button at the top, raises his fist in triumph, and drops off the wall. His safety line catches him and lowers him to the ground where his friends surround him.

They clap him on the back and congratulate him before the whole group of boys goes off to another climbing route on the other side of the gym.

I take the opportunity to scan the gym on my left and right. I realize a second too late that I'm looking for Jayden. He would be here if he wasn't trying to take me to court for custody of my son.

I still feel fragile about all that, but the last couple of days have somewhat softened the anguish. Now I just hate the fuck out of him.

I want to kill him and I can't stop staying up late at night trying to find a way to beat this motion. I still haven't found one, but I'll never stop looking. There has to be a way to stop it before the unthinkable happens.

Someone grabs my arm and I whip around the other way to find one of the mothers from Kai's school smiling at me. "Hi! How are you? Kai's climbing is getting so much better! He can beat Will now. He could never do that before."

"Yeah. He's great."

"Hey!" she blurts out. "Will's birthday is weekend after next. We were thinking about taking the boys to a lake for a sleep-over-slash-campout. What do you think? Could Kai come?"

"That would be awesome. I'm sure he'd love it. Text me all the information, okay? Do you have my number?"

We exchange numbers. At least Kai can keep having a normal life until Jayden pulls the rug out from underneath his feet.

She leaves me alone with my depressing thoughts and I turn back to watch Kai. He's the light of my life.... or he will be until he isn't anymore. I can't even enjoy these good times with the ax hanging over my head.

I turn to talk about my troubles to the one person I've always relied on for that, but Jayden isn't here. Jayden is the one doing this to me—to both of us. What am I going to do?

I can't keep turning to him and coming up empty, but he's my only support. None of my other friends understand.

I could never tell Harper about any of this. She's way too wrapped up in her own problems and she isn't interested in having kids. She would probably tell me that I should be glad someone is taking Kai off my hands.

My stomach hurts when I think about someone actually saying that. My stomach has been hurting a lot these last few days. I'm going to make myself permanently sick if this worry keeps eating me away from the inside.

Kai comes running toward me and we leave the wall for the concession stand. We get hot dogs and sit down at the picnic table to sip our soda and watch the other climbers.

"Will's mom mentioned you going on his birthday sleepover at the lake weekend after next," I tell him. "You cool with that?"

"Yeah!" he exclaims. "That sounds great."

"You're getting to be a really good climber. Why don't we plan a trip to go out to Helix Canyon over summer vacation? We could camp out there for a week or two and climb. What do you say?"

He starts to grin and then his face falls. His eyes skip sideways at nothing. "Mom?"

"Yeah, sweetie? What is it? We don't have to go to Helix Canyon if you don't want to. We can go somewhere else."

"It isn't that. It's just…. Jayden said he wanted to take me horse trekking over summer vacation with Stuart and his kids. That sounds fun…. too. Maybe I could do both."

I compress my lips. I need to make an effort not to criticize Jayden in front of Kai, but I can't help but get annoyed. Jayden is already causing me enough problems and now he's going behind my back and filling Kai's head with all these wild ideas and plans that haven't even been made yet.

I don't have a problem with Jayden taking Kai on trips with his new cousins. Hell, I won't be able to stop Jayden from doing exactly that once the adoption gets nullified.

That's the problem. I'm more upset about the motion to vacate the adoption than with anything else Jayden has done or has proposed to do. I could cope with anything if it wasn't for that damn motion.

"Mom?" Kai's voice sounds tiny and so….so childlike. "I miss Jayden."

I gulp down the lump in my throat. "I miss him, too, sweetie."

"He would be here right now if this wasn't going on. He was always here on Saturdays."

"I know, darling. I wish everything could just go back to the way things were before."

"Isn't there any way you can work it out with him? He said at school that he wanted to."

"I don't know, sweetie. It's kind of hard to trust anything he says now."

"Can't you at least try? How are you supposed to know if you can work it out with him if you don't even talk to him?"

I look up into my son's eyes—Jayden's eyes. Kai looks so sad and so scared about this whole thing. He's been going about his business like I told him to, but he lets his feelings show every now and then.

I want to cry when I see how much this is bothering him. Is he getting a sore stomach worrying about this, too? I would do anything to spare him that.

I say I would do anything, but does that include compromising with Jayden? Can I really take that step? I don't want to. I never want to see him again for the rest of my life. I want him to die a slow, painful death for doing this.

If Jenny is right and there's nothing I can do to stop this motion from being granted, then compromising with Jayden is the only way I'll ever be able to see Kai. If Jayden wins this motion the way Jenny thinks he will, never seeing Jayden will mean never seeing Kai. I can't let that happen.

I have to compromise with him or at least offer the olive branch. Maybe he'll be reasonable. He wouldn't offer to come to some agreement if he just wanted to take Kai and shut me out completely.

"I'll try, sweetie," I tell him. "You go back to climbing and I'll see what I can do."

Kai runs off and I pull out my phone. I stare at the screen warring with all the emotions threatening to tear me apart. What am I supposed to say to Jayden? Am I supposed to beg him to let me stay in Kai's life? I can't swallow my pride enough to say that.

I start to put my phone away when it buzzes in my hand. The name pops up on the screen and I stiffen. *Jayden Aldrich.* What does he want?

I flick open the text. *Would it be all right if I hang out with you and Kai? I miss you guys. Are you at the climbing gym?*

My scalp prickles. I don't want to hang out with him, but my conversation with Kai comes back to me. What better time to start than now?

I start typing rapidly. *I don't know how to deal with you now and I think I might be getting an ulcer from having to face this motion to vacate the adoption. I don't think it's a good idea for us to hang out under the circumstances.*

He takes an extra minute before he answers. *I'm sorry to hear that. I never meant for it to bother you that much. I'm serious about us sharing time with Kai and working this out so it benefits all of us, especially him. I understand that staying with you is the best thing for him. I just want to be the father he deserves and that means I should be in his life, too. Surely you can understand that.*

I clamp my eyes shut. I don't want to listen, but I know he's right. *How exactly do you suggest we work it out?*

I'd rather talk about it in person if it's all the same to you. If you don't want me to come to the gym, I won't. I won't intrude on your relationship with Kai, but I think we should make another time when we can meet and talk about it.

Damn it. Why does he have to be so reasonable about this? He makes it impossible to stay mad at him. *Fine. We're at the gym.*

Does that mean you're okay with me coming over?

Okay. Kai wants to see you anyway.

Thank you, Quinn. I'm grateful. I know this motion is hard on you. If we work it out, maybe it doesn't have to be.

I need to get out of this conversation. *I'll talk to you when you get here.*

I put my phone in my pocket, but I can't even enjoy watching Kai anymore. My stomach tightens painfully thinking about seeing Jayden again. I don't want to do this, but it looks like I have no choice.

Chapter 14: Jayden

My pulse races walking up to the climbing gym entrance. I've been here a thousand times with Quinn and Kai, but this time takes on a whole new meaning. This will be the first time I've been here as Kai's father—his dad.

He actually called me that. My whole life is changing with that word ringing in my ears. I'm something so much more than his father. I'm his dad.

I want the whole world with him, but I understand now that he has to stay with Quinn. Taking him away from her wouldn't be the best thing for him. I just have to find a way to work things out with her so we can all move on and start enjoying our lives.

I'm not sure I'm ready to deal with her, either. I don't know how to think about her anymore. We definitely aren't friends anymore. I never thought I'd live to see the day when we wouldn't be, but this situation sure as hell drove a stake through our friendship's heart.

I find it hard to breathe as I walk through the entrance doors. I spot her right away and she levels me with one of her death stares when I get nearer to the climbing area. This should be interesting if we get into another massive fight right here in public.

Just then, Kai calls out from high on the nearest wall. "Jayden!" He waves down at me and lets go of the holds before he reaches the top.

He grins like a banshee gliding down to the ground and he charges over to me. He collides with me and throws his arms around me. "You came! Come on, Jayden! I'm climbing all the way to the top of the big pyramid. Put your shoes on and come on!"

I shoot a glance at Quinn, but she still doesn't move. She doesn't intervene to stop me from climbing with Kai. We always climb together, so why should she interfere now?

"Okay, buddy. Hang on and let me pay first."

He bounces around me talking a mile a minute while I pay my entrance fee and lace up my climbing shoes. He goes ballistic when I finally stand up and follow him to the giant inverted pyramid in the center of the climbing cage.

Quinn's eyes drill into the back of my head when Kai and I swing onto the wall. "Twenty bragging points for whoever gets to the top first!" I call over to Kai.

"You're on!" He starts climbing faster. He really has gotten better since he started coming here last year.

I push myself harder, but he keeps up and starts to pull ahead. "You better hurry up, slowpoke!" he calls and then laughs at me when I miss my next handhold.

I grit my teeth, but he's already putting more distance between us. Seeing me fall behind gives him new energy and he shoots upward at impossible speed. "No way!" I yell as he hits the button. "You little sneak!"

Kai laughs out loud and I find myself joining in. I had all but given up on ever sharing these moments with him again.

I catch myself glancing down at Quinn to see if she's enjoying this as much as I am. She's smiling, but the minute I make eye contact with her, the same glint of malice flashes across her face.

I spend the next ten minutes crawling all over the gym with Kai. If I can't work things out with her, I can start building my future relationship with him at the very least.

I finally sail down to the floor after another defeat at the hands of my eight-year-old son. This is a preview of things to come. He'll keep getting stronger and faster and more confident while he leaves me in the dust.

"Great climbing, buddy," I tell him when he comes over to me from the parallel course. "I must be getting old."

He laughs. "Come on, Jayden! Let's do the boulders again!"

"You go on and climb with your friends. I gotta talk to your mom."

His delighted smile evaporates immediately and he casts a worried glance at her. "Do you think you can work things out with her?"

"I hope so. I'll try, anyway. You go on and leave it to me."

"Okay." He gives me another quick hug. He's been doing that a lot more since he found out. He wants this as much as I do. I can't let him down.

He runs off. That's my cue to go face the firing squad. I leave the cage and sit down on the bench to take off my climbing shoes before I head over to meet Quinn.

She leaves the fence while I'm untying my shoes, but she doesn't come over and sit down next to me like she usually would. She stands off to one side and eyes me with her arms crossed over her chest.

I finally straighten up and work up the courage to go over to her. "Do you want to sit down at the picnic tables?" I ask.

She looks away. "I guess."

"Would you rather stand?" I ask.

"I really don't care."

She isn't making this any easier for me. I take another deep breath. "We're both here and we both know we need to talk about this, so let's talk about it. I'm not trying to take Kai away from you."

"Why didn't you just work with me from the beginning then? Why did you have to file that motion at all? The motion sure makes it look like you're trying to take him away from me."

"I tried to work with you at the beginning. Don't you remember? I tried to talk to you about working out a custody arrangement and you went off and started screaming at me. You said I wasn't his father and that I was a stranger. What was I supposed to do? I can't let you push me out of his life."

"You didn't have to file that motion. If you really care about him at all, you'll withdraw it."

"I can't do that," I tell her. "I want to be declared his legal father so he can be included in my family. He'll stand to inherit our property the same way his cousins do. I hate to say this, but I also need to do this to assert my parental rights so you won't be able to cut me off if I do something you don't like. I have to protect myself and my relationship with him. I'm sorry, but that's just the way it has to be."

She doesn't answer and she won't look at me. She pretends to watch Kai climbing with his friends.

"I'm sorry, Quinn. I never meant to hurt you, but this is more important than our friendship. You know that as well as I do. If I have to choose between Kai and our friendship, there's no contest."

"I know that," she finally mutters. "I feel the same way about him."

"Come on," I murmur under my breath. "Let's work this out. You're his mother and I'm his father so we're both going to be stuck with each other for a long, long time. We need to get along and decide what's best for him."

She glances over at me for a fraction of a second. "Were you serious about him staying with me? Did you really mean that?"

"Of course!" I breathe. "I don't want to hurt him.... or you."

"Well, you did hurt me. You hurt me with that motion."

"There is a way we can get around this, you know," I murmur even lower. "There's a way we can both be his legal parents."

"How?"

"We get married."

She whips around fast and gasps. "What?! No!! How can you even suggest that?"

"We both love Kai and we both want what's best for him. What's best for him is to have both his parents in one house married to each other. That's you and me. This is the best way to give him the home he needs. You know it and I know it."

"I do not know it!" she snaps. "I'm not marrying you, especially after the shit you pulled on me....and him! How could you even suggest that?"

"I'm trying to find a solution to your mutual problem. You said you wanted the same thing. It's the one solution that solves every part of the problem. It means we both have equal rights as his parents. It means neither of us can take him away from the other and it means that he doesn't have to bounce back and forth between two different homes. What could be better than that?"

She keeps her head turned stubbornly away from me.

"Come on, Quinn!" I urge. "You know this is what he wants. You know he wants us both and what better way to do that than for us to be together?"

"You're only saying that to get into my pants again," she growls.

My hackles rise at those words. "Are you trying to make me mad? Are you trying to piss me off so bad that I walk out that door right now? Is that what you really want? Turn around and look at me. I'm not fucking around here, Quinn. You turn around right now or I walk. That's my final word."

She turns around and glares at me with plenty of her old hostility, but the longer she stands there, the more she wilts. She finally shakes her hair out of her eyes and looks down at the ground. "Sorry. I shouldn't have said that."

"We're both on the same side here, Quinn," I tell her. "I'm not your enemy."

"I can't marry you. Even if I thought there was a chance once—which I didn't—that's all gone now. I don't know if I can even trust you anymore."

"Okay. So us getting married is out. So what's next?"

"There's nothing next." Her voice starts to quaver and her eyes fill up with tears. "You're going to vacate the adoption and I'm going to be left out in the cold."

"I would never do that, Quinn. I care too much about Kai and I care about you. If we don't get married, we'll just share custody. That's all there is to it."

"We won't share custody because I won't have any rights. I'll be the stranger. I'll be nothing. I won't even be his mother anymore."

Her face spasms and she curls her lips into her mouth, but nothing can stop the tears. She turns away toward the climbing walls and wipes the tears off her cheeks, but nothing can stop them.

I can't stand that. I shouldn't presume, but I have to put my arms around her. I want to promise her that I'll withdraw the motion, but I can't do that. I have my own responsibilities as a father now. I have to do what's right for Kai.

She doesn't try to stop me from hugging her or even from kissing her on the head. There has to be a way to stop this from happening, but she's right. There is no going back.

Chapter 15: Jayden

I have to fight down nerves when Quinn and her lawyer step into the negotiation room at the county courthouse Family Court Arbitration Unit. This is the last stop before we take this motion to vacate before a judge.

If that happens, it's all she wrote for Quinn as Kai's mother. My lawyer, Tim Hartley, has been over this and over this with his legal team. Tim is iron-clad certain our case is in the bag, but I'm starting to have serious doubts about whether I can go through with this.

Tim shakes hands with Jenny Warren and then with Quinn. "Thank you for meeting us, Ms. Brown," he tells Quinn. "Take a seat and let's talk this thing out."

"Does your client still intend to push this motion through?" Jenny asks.

"My client doesn't intend to push anything through anything," Tim replies. "My client simply wishes to have his legal rights asserted. This adoption is totally invalid as I'm sure both you and your client can understand. My client's pregnant wife fled the state, gave birth on the opposite coast without his knowledge, and then abandoned his son in state custody before she died in an alley. My client has every right to want his son back. We apologize for the inconvenience to your client, but...."

"Inconvenience!" Quinn snarls. "You call raising a child for eight years, working around the clock seven days a week and giving this child the best years of my life an inconvenience? How would your client like to compensate me for eight years of lost wages, lost sleep, and emotional distress just as an added bonus?"

Tim doesn't bat an eyelash. "I'm sure my client would inform you that he had nothing to do with any of that and the person you should be seeking compensation from is his deceased wife. She was the one who caused this, not my client."

Quinn winds up for another assault, but at that moment, the door opens and another man walks in. He strolls over to Tim and Tim stands up to shake his hand. "Thank you for coming over. I appreciate it."

"What is the meaning of this?" Jenny demands. "This is a closed negotiation."

"This is Charles Keating," Tim replies. "I asked him to come. Mr. Keating, this is the respondent, Quinn Brown, and her attorney, Jenny Warren."

Keating extends his hand across the table, but neither Quinn nor Jenny gets up to greet him. "What are you doing here?" Jenny snaps. "Unless you have something to add to this negotiation...."

"There is no negotiation," Keating replies. "I'm a social worker with Child Protective Services for the State of Washington. We've been in contact with our counterparties in Oregon and we've vacated the adoption from our end."

"YOU WHAT??!!" Quinn roars.

Keating puts a zippered nylon folder on the desk, opens it, and starts pulling out papers. "The adoption has been declared null and void. I'm here to supervise immediate transfer of custody of the boy to his father."

"No!!" Quinn yells and then breaks down in hysterics. "No, you can't! You can't take him away from me! You said you wouldn't, Jayden! You can't do this! You can't take my son! Jayden, you promised!"

She starts to get out of her chair. Jenny tries to hold her back, but there's no stopping Quinn now. Her voice spikes to a shriek. "No!! You can't take him away from me!! You can't do this!! I won't let you!! Jayden, you promised me you wouldn't take him away!!"

She tries to lunge for Keating and Jenny barely grabs her in time to hold Quinn back.

"Mr. Aldrich had nothing to do with this," Keating goes on. "The order to vacate came from the state level. If Mr. Aldrich refuses to assume custody of the boy, I'm under orders from the Ninth Circuit Court to investigate transferring custody to Mr. Aldrich's next nearest relative."

Quinn stares at him in horrified shock. Tears pour from her eyes, but she's so floored that she can't even scream anymore. My stomach turns looking at her. "Isn't there any way to reverse this?" I ask. "Isn't there any way for us to share custody or something?"

"Unfortunately not," Keating replies. "Ms. Brown's parental claim rested on a fraudulent premise that the boy had no known relatives. His mother had no legal right to relinquish custody on your behalf, therefore your rights are asserted and the adoption is void."

Quinn gives one excruciating hiccup of sobs, rips herself out of Jenny's arms, and charges from the room, screaming, "I'll never let you take him away from me! Never!"

The door slams shut and Jenny collapses into her chair. She buries her face in her hands. "How could you do this, Jayden? How could you do this to her of all people?"

I want to puke or maybe start crying myself. All this talk about working it out with her—all this talk about doing what's right for Kai by keeping them together—it doesn't mean squat.

Keating pushes a stack of papers toward Tim. "Here is all the relevant documentation of the judge's decision and here's my card. You can call me or the Seattle office if you have any questions."

"What's going to happen to Kai?" I ask.

"I'm empowered to stay in town for a month to ensure a smooth transfer of custody," Keating tells me. "If Ms. Brown resists or causes any trouble or refuses to hand the boy over, our office and the local branch of CPS will handle it. There's no need for you to muddy the waters by getting involved."

"Muddy the waters?" I repeat. "The waters are already as muddy as they're going to get."

He zips his folder closed. It sounds extra loud in the silence. He walks out and leaves me standing there with my heart in my shoes. How did this happen?

"Well, that's all taken care of." Tim takes Keating's papers. "Unless there's anything else, Ms. Warren...."

I can't listen to this. I need to find Quinn. I need to do something about this. I'm the only person who can.

I walk out of the room without a word and look up and down the hall. She has to be here somewhere. She's too responsible to drive when she's this upset and she won't do anything stupid like take Kai on the run. That threat was just her way of expressing how devastated she is.

This is the worst possible outcome I can imagine, but in a way, it was inevitable that the state would intervene as soon as they realized their mistake. I just have to find Quinn and....do something. Don't ask me what.

I head off down the corridor searching every open room. I pass the women's bathroom and dare to stick my head in. I might get arrested for this, but I just don't care at this point.

I don't hear any crying in there, so I go back the way I came. I finally go into the stairwell to search the lower levels and find her sobbing in a corner.

She stands with her forehead pressed into the cold concrete where the two walls meet. Her whole body quakes with racking sobs. It hurts just to look at her.

I put my arms around her from behind. "I'm so sorry, baby!" I whisper in her ear. "I'm so sorry!"

She explodes in torturous sobs and my throat constricts. My eyes sting listening to her. I never would have done this to her if I had known it would come to this. I never wanted any of this to happen.

She suddenly revolts at my touch, throws an elbow back at me to drive me off, and roars out one animal bellow of pain and anguish. She rotates halfway around to make sure I back away, and in that moment, I get a good look at the catastrophe that is her face.

This is a thousand times worse than listening to her cry. I catch her before she turns away and I hold her tight when she tries to struggle out of my arms. I have to hold onto her. I have to be there to help her even though I'm the one who's inflicting this pain on her.

She wrenches a few more times in my embrace before she collapses in excruciating sobs. Her forehead falls on my chest and I wind up crying into her hair. I can't hold back how much this hurts. I can't let this happen to her. I don't care what it costs. I have to make this right.

She cries for a good fifteen minutes before she straightens up. She doesn't even try to hide her blotchy, swollen face from me and her eyes still stream with tears. "Go away, Jayden," she husks. "Just leave me alone."

She immediately starts crying again, but I don't let her fall apart a second time. I grab her arms and struggle not to shake her. "Listen to me, sweetheart. There's a way to stop this. We can't stop the custody transfer, but there's a way to keep you and Kai together. I'm going to move into your apartment—right now—today. We don't have to get married and we don't have to get involved and we don't have to screw around. We're friends or at least in the same boat together. If I move into your apartment, no one can say I'm not taking custody of him, but you two will still be together. You'll still be his mother. You'll always be his mother. We'll be there together and we'll parent him together. It's the best solution. It's the only solution."

"Forget it," she growls and starts to turn away.

I don't let her go. I tighten my grip on her arms. I can't tell if I'm holding her too tightly. I might even be hurting her, but it doesn't matter anymore. I have to convince her. This is our last chance.

"Do you want to lose him? Do you want the state to take him away from you? If I refuse to take custody, they'll give him to Eva or my mother or someone else. It has to be me and the only way for you to keep him is for me to move into your apartment. There's no question. We're doing this. There's no other way around it."

She raises her scarlet eyes to me. She looks absolutely awful, but she doesn't argue.

"I made you a promise not to take him away from you and I plan to keep it. He's staying with you and this is the way we're going to do it."

She sniffs and looks down at the ground. "Okay."

I put my arms around her and kiss the side of her head. She doesn't fight me off, but she doesn't hug me back, either. I don't know what's going to happen between us, but I know this is right. I've never been more certain of anything.

I straighten up and look down at her. She looks somewhat calmer and she isn't crying anymore. She just looks like she just went nine rounds with a heavyweight boxer. "What's going to happen now?" she croaks.

"You're going to go out to the parking lot, get in your car, and go home so you're there when Kai gets home from school. I'm going to talk to Tim and Jenny. I'll tell them that I'm taking custody of Kai as of tonight so they can close this case and Tim can withdraw my motion to vacate. Then I'm going to go to my apartment and pack up a few things to bring over for tonight. I'll meet you back at your place at about six o'clock and we'll talk to Kai about what's happening so he understands. Then, probably in the next week, I'll clean out my apartment, put it up for rent, and change my address so your place will be my official residence. Once I do that, I'll contact this Keating guy and we'll set a day and a time when he can come over and make sure I'm taking custody of Kai at my new official residence."

"What will you tell him about me?"

"He doesn't have to know. You can go take a walk around the block or go out to lunch before he comes over. He'll see me living there with Kai and he can go back to Washington satisfied that everything's hunky-dory. He doesn't have to know we're living together."

Her eyes dart up to my face. "Are you sure about this?"

"Of course I'm sure. I told you I would never take him away from you. I had no idea any of this was going to happen. I came here today thinking we would come up with some kind of shared time arrangement, but if that isn't possible, then we have to do it this way."

"Thanks," she mumbles.

I have to hug her. I have to kiss her hair. "I would never knowingly hurt you like this, sweetheart. I love you. I love you both."

She doesn't answer, and when I let her go, I push her away toward the exit. "Go get in your car and go home. Kai needs you. I'll see you in a little while."

She gives me one more pained look and walks away. Now I just have to get busy completely rearranging my life. I'm about to become a father in a whole new way.

Chapter 16: Quinn

I sit on the couch smashing my hands between my knees to stop them from shaking. I can't stop rocking back and forth in agitation as I count down the seconds until Kai comes home from school.

My whole body aches from the strain and my stomach feels like someone is stabbing me in the guts. The adoption is null and void. Kai isn't mine anymore.

Jayden is my only hope now. I don't want to trust him, but I have to. Maybe I misjudged him if he came up with this solution so quickly. He's moving into my apartment so I can keep parenting Kai.

I want to start crying again, but I can't do that. I need to pull myself together real fast. Kai will be here in a few minutes and then Jayden will come over—for good. He'll move in with us and he'll start being a father to Kai. Can I live with that? I have no choice.

This inexpressible gratitude to him keeps overwhelming my desire to hate him. I want to push him out of my life, but I can't now and not because he's letting me keep Kai. I couldn't push Jayden out of my life after what he's doing for me. I owe him too much. I owe him everything. I owe him my very life.

What am I going to say to Kai? He'll know something's up the instant he sees me. I'll just have to tell him the truth as simply and straightforwardly as I can. I'll just have to bite the bullet. There's no discussion, no question. Jayden is right about that.

The elevator pings and Kai's footsteps come down the corridor outside. I force myself to stop rocking and to put my hands on my knees so he won't see what a mess I am, although he'll be able to see when he sees my face.

He walks in and his expression changes instantly. He looks scared. I can't have that. I need to put his mind at rest right away. I can't let him live with the stress any longer.

"Mom?" he asks. "What's wrong?"

"Come here, sweetie. Sit down. I need to talk to you."

He comes over to the couch and looks up at me with that horrified look like I'm about to devastate his world again.

I take his hand and squeeze. "I had a meeting today with Jayden and his lawyer and my lawyer where we talked about who you're going to live with."

"Yeah?" he asks. "Is Jayden going to take me away from you?"

"No, sweetie." I fight back tears. "Jayden is going to come and live with us here. I'm going to keep being your mom and he's going to be your dad and we're going to live together. I don't know how long it will last, but we're going to try our best to make it work for as long as we can. We both want what's best for you and this is what's best for you so that's what we're going to do."

He stares at me blinking extra slowly. "Seriously? For real?"

I nod. "Yeah. He's coming over later and he'll probably have dinner with us. I guess...." I glance up the stairs. "I guess he'll stay in the guest room."

Kai bursts into one of his huge, beaming grins. "This is so great! This is perfect! Why couldn't you just do that to begin with? Jayden is over here all the time anyways. This is awesome!" He jumps up laughing, grabs his backpack, and takes off for the stairs. "I can't wait until he comes over!"

He tears away to his room and I hear him banging around with his stuff. I should have known he'd be in heaven over this deal. I'm the only one who has a problem with it.

I'm not getting any more okay with it by sitting here. Thinking about Jayden coming over and moving in here just makes me more anxious.

I need to make dinner anyway, so I get up and go to the kitchen. Doing something helps me calm down. It always does. It always helps me get over every problem I've ever faced since Max died. I just keep moving, making the food, putting Kai to bed, taking him to school—all the millions of tasks that have to be done to manage our lives.

I just have to keep moving now. Tonight will pass, and eventually, Jayden living here will become normal. I can't imagine that now, but when I remember how it was when Jayden and I were only friends, it doesn't seem so far-fetched.

He's a good man. He must be if he's doing this for me. He's doing it for Kai, but he's also doing it for me. I can believe him when he says he never meant to hurt me like this.

He could have just taken Kai and left me with nothing. He doesn't have to do this. I'm beyond grateful that he's doing it. I'm just still so wound up about it that I can't think beyond the moment right now.

I get busy making dinner, and while I'm doing it, I get some work-related emails. I get distracted by that and by the rest of my normal evening routine until five-thirty when Kai comes downstairs.

"When is Jayden coming over?" he asks.

I snap out of my thoughts. Jayden is coming over. "He said six. I better straighten up the guest room for him. Could you set the table for dinner, sweetheart?"

I hurry upstairs. No one has slept in the guest room....well, ever. I strip the bed and put on all clean bedding. I whizz around the room trying to make everything super perfectly perfect. I don't know why. Jayden already knows what my house is like.

I get back downstairs to find Kai working his fingers to the bone to set the table much fancier than we've ever set it before. Jayden has eaten dinner with us millions of times, but now Kai takes extra special care to make sure every fork and napkin is in exactly the right position.

He's working on place cards when Jayden knocks on the door at the stroke of six. Kai drops his cards and scissors and charges the door. He gets there before me, rips it off its hinges, and drags Jayden in. "You don't have to knock. You're living here now."

Jayden carries a loaded duffel bag over one shoulder. He has to drop it by the door when Kai lays hold of him and Jayden glances over at me. "I guess your mom broke the news."

"You sit here, Jayden." Kai shoves him into a seat. "I'm just finishing the place cards."

"Are you going to make place cards every night?" Jayden calls after him and then shoots me a smirk on the side.

I stand at the kitchen counter trying like crazy to figure out what I'm supposed to do. Why am I acting so unnerved by him? Him being here shouldn't be any different, but it is. Everything is different now.

Kai starts laying out his place cards and the timer on the oven goes off. I take the food out and put it on a hot pad in the middle of the table. My pulse quickens when I get too near Jayden. I shouldn't be getting unsettled by him being here, but I can't help it.

Those basic movements get me back into the groove of going through my routine. I have to keep doing what I always do to take care of Kai whether Jayden is here or not.

I switch off the oven and take my seat. This feels more natural now that I'm sitting here and seeing Kai and Jayden across from me in the places where they've been so many times before. Maybe this isn't so different from the way it was before.

Kai kicks things off with his usual childlike simplicity. "How long are you staying here, Jayden?"

"I don't know. I guess we'll just play it by ear and see what happens. Let's put it this way. I'll stay here as long as you need me to."

"It's gonna be so great having you here," Kai goes on. "Now I don't have to wait for you to come over. We can talk whenever we want."

"Yeah." Jayden gazes at him across the table and Kai gazes back. "It's gonna be great."

Kai keeps talking about all the stuff they're going to do together. Kai has Jayden's whole schedule planned out. I don't think Kai realizes that Jayden has a business to run and won't be here around the clock.

I can already see the chemistry between these two. They can't get enough of each other, now that they both know they have no reason to hold each other at arm's length. They're a dream come true for each other.

Jayden really is the best thing for Kai. I shouldn't have been so quick to defend my patch. I should have been more willing to cooperate with Jayden.

Kai is still talking in an endless stream of ideas when I stand up and take the leftovers to the fridge. "Go upstairs and get your homework," I tell him. "You can bring it down here and get started on it."

"Aw, Mom! I'm in the middle of explaining my new death ray invention."

"Jayden was really good at math when he was in school. Maybe he can help you do your homework."

Kai stares at Jayden in awe. "You were good at math?"

"It was a long time ago, but yeah. I still do it a lot for my business. Go get your homework and let's take a look."

I fade into the background and listen to Jayden helping Kai with his homework while I clean the kitchen. Jayden really is good with Kai and Kai listens to Jayden much better than he listens to me. Kai needs a father or at least another adult to interact with.

Kai has always responded to Jayden, but never like this. Kai actually pays attention when Jayden explains something instead of getting frustrated and giving up in annoyance.

I do everything possible to stay out of it until I absolutely have to. I go over and put my hand on Kai's shoulder. "It's time for you to get ready for bed. Put your homework away, brush your teeth, and get into your pajamas. Don't argue! If you finish quickly, you can talk to Jayden before you go to bed."

Kai takes off and Jayden looks up at me....with *that* look. What is he thinking that for? We're doing this as a business arrangement for Kai—nothing more.

He opens his mouth like he's about to say something. I don't want to hear whatever it is so I cut him off. "Why don't you bring your duffel bag upstairs? You can stay in the guest room."

He picks it up, follows me upstairs, and puts his bag on the bed in the guest room. He turns in a circle looking at everything like he's never seen this room before because hasn't.

He turns around and his eyes smolder when he looks at me. "Thank you for doing this."

"Why are you thanking me? I should be the one thanking you. It was either this or lose Kai."

"I mean...."

Just then, Kai yells from down the stairs behind me.

"I'm in here!" Jayden calls out and quickly strides past me into the hall.

A second later, I hear him and Kai go into Kai's bedroom. I go through another flurry of confusion about what to do with myself now that Jayden is staying in my apartment. I don't want to go downstairs in case Jayden comes down there and gets some idea about us hooking up the way we did last time.

I make a snap decision, go downstairs, switch off all the lights, and retreat to my room. I don't feel right about shutting the door and barricading myself inside to defend myself against Jayden, so I leave the door open praying to High Heaven that he'll get the message and not come around trying to talk to me.

I shouldn't be working this hard to avoid him, but his presence makes me so uncomfortable that I have to. I have to do something to get over this initial awkward stage before I get used to him being here.

I sit down on my bed and start doing some work on my phone. I have some catching up to do. My brain has been shot these last several days over this whole motion to vacate Kai's adoption.

There is no way in Holy Hell I'm letting Jayden pay for Kai. I'm not doing this for Jayden's money which means I need to keep making a living.

I can't help hearing their voices coming from Kai's room. They talk in low tones in an almost intimate way that grips my heart. I've been the only one to share those precious moments right before Kai goes to sleep. I've been the one he confides in.

Now Jayden is taking my place. I shouldn't be getting emotional about losing those beautiful times. Jayden has missed out on eight years of those moments thanks to Helena.

Mr. Keating is right. She's the one who did this. None of this is Jayden's fault. I should be glad that he wants to be so involved in Kai's life. I should be thrilled and grateful that both Kai and Jayden can start treating each other this way so quickly.

I am grateful for it and I'm glad Kai can have that with Jayden. I just wish.....I can't bring myself to wish that Jayden wasn't coming between me and Kai because he isn't.

If Max was alive, he and I would have raised Kai together. Max would have been talking to Kai in his room at least as much as I was. Max would be the one talking to Kai like this right now.

I wouldn't resent him for that. I have no reason to resent Jayden and I don't. I just need this one night to get my head screwed on straight about what I'm doing and why.

I go to the bathroom half an hour later and see Jayden sitting on the edge of Kai's bed in exactly the place where I usually sit when I put Kai to bed. Kai is all tucked in with the covers over his chest. He looks up at Jayden with exactly the same expression he usually uses to look at me. Kai really is looking at Jayden like Jayden is Kai's dad.

I go back to my room and their voices get quieter and quieter until Jayden walks out of Kai's room and shuts the door. Jayden doesn't come toward my room. He goes into the guest room and shuts that door. He doesn't even try to say goodnight to me.

Now I'm truly alone. I have nothing to do but shut my door and go to bed. I got everything I wanted. I got to keep my son. No one will take him away from me, so why do I feel so sad?

Chapter 17: Jayden

I come out of the guest room on my way downstairs, but when I pass Kai's room and see him sitting on the floor, I change my mind.

I go in there and find him working on one of his crazy inventions. He's taken the cardboard egg carton out of the recycling bin and attached a bunch of wooden popsicle sticks to the different cups. I can't even figure out what it is and I make an executive decision not to ask.

"Hey, buddy," I begin. "You remember when I told you about Eva and Stuart taking Simon and Andrea on a horse trekking trip this summer vacation? Do you still want to go? I'm booking our airfare right now. What do you say?"

"Yeah! That would be great!" His face falls. "Except that Mom said we would go climbing at Helix Canyon. She wants us to camp out and climb during summer vacation."

"Well, summer vacation is pretty long. Maybe we could do both."

His eyes fall out of their sockets. "Really?" He frowns again and looks toward the door. "What will Mom say?"

"I'll ask her. I'll convince her to let you go. Besides, she can come with us if she wants to. She likes horseback riding."

"She does? She never said anything about it."

Sure," I tell him. "She used to ride at the estate all the time when we were growing up. She never went trekking with us, but she likes to ride. She's pretty good, too."

He won't stop gawking at me. "No way!"

"So do you want to go if she says yes?"

"Absolutely!" he exclaims. "How long will we go for? Where are we going? Do we have to do anything with the horses? What if I'm not as good a rider as Andrea and Simon? Do they have special horses for beginners?"

"Stuart and Eva are going for a week, so we'll see about airfares and maybe stay in a hotel before we leave for the...."

I trail off when Quinn appears in the doorway. She leans against the doorjamb and crosses her arms.

"Mom!" Kai blurts out. "Jayden's taking me horse trekking with Andrea and Simon and Eva and Stuart! Isn't that cool? We're gonna fly in a plane and everything!"

"Is that so?" Her eyes slice over to me. "What happened to climbing in Helix Canyon?"

"He says we could do both. He says you could come trekking with us. He says you used to ride horses when you were younger. Is that true, Mom? Hey! Jayden could come to Helix Canyon with us! He likes climbing. Come on, Mom! Say yes."

She looks back and forth between us and finally says, "Okay. You can go," before she walks off.

Kai and I exchange glances. She didn't sound happy about that.

Kai bends over his invention and doesn't look up again. Now it's my turn to grab the bull by the horns.

I go after her, but she's hiding in her room again. At least she left the door open.

She's busy rummaging in her drawers and pretends not to see me when I take the same position leaning against the doorjamb so she won't think I'm invading her territory.

"Do you have an issue with me taking Kai horse trekking with his cousins? If you do, tell me now so we can talk about it."

"I don't have an issue with it," she replies without turning around.

"You're acting like you do."

"Why would I have an issue with it? They're his cousins. Why shouldn't he spend time with them over summer vacation?"

She spins around fast and barges past me heading down the hall on her way to the stairs. Now I know this is bothering her.

I tail her downstairs and corner her in the laundry room. "Why are you acting so hostile about this? I suggested that you come with us. I don't see why you're so opposed to it. I've done everything to accommodate your wishes. I don't know what else I can do besides not take him out, but I'm not going to do that."

"I'm not opposed to it. I just wish you would talk to me about it first before you talk to him. If you tell him and get his hopes up, then it puts me in a difficult position where I can't disapprove without looking like the bad guy."

I shrug. "Okay. I'm sorry. I should have thought of that. So.... if you don't disapprove, why are you so hostile to the idea of me taking him out?"

"I'm not hostile about that."

"You could have fooled me. You won't talk to me or even hardly look at me since I moved in here. You won't stay alone in the same room with me. What am I supposed to think?"

"I have no idea what you're supposed to think."

I smack my lips in annoyance. "Oh, come on, Quinn. You can't possibly think that this simmering tension between us all the time is what's best for Kai. Don't you think he can see this yawning chasm of antagonism between us?"

She hesitates a split second, and at that moment, Kai calls from the living room. "Mom! I'm going downstairs to Frank's apartment. I want to show him my invention."

"Okay, sweetie!" she calls. "Be home for dinner."

We both hold our breath and listen until he leaves and shuts the apartment door behind him. Now we're alone together.

She reacts instantly by shoving me aside and walking away again. I'm getting really sick and tired of this.

I walk after her fast to catch up with her. "If you don't have a problem with me taking him over summer vacation, you must not have a problem with me taking him to the estate next weekend to meet Simon and Andrea."

She whips around fast. "Why didn't you tell me this before?"

"I'm telling you now. I haven't mentioned it to him. This is the first time I've mentioned it to anyone except for Stuart when I asked him to meet us there."

She compresses her lips, doesn't answer, and heads off toward her bedroom, but I'm all done playing games. I won't let her hide from me anymore. "You can't keep walking away from me, Quinn. I'm in this as Kai's other parent. You're going to have to deal with me sooner or later."

"Fine," she snaps over her shoulder. "Take him to the estate. I don't have a problem with that."

"Come with us. Come have lunch with me and my family."

She rounds on me in her bedroom door. "What the hell for—so you can keep pretending that we're getting married? Give it up, Jayden."

"We don't have to tell them we're getting married."

"You already did! If I go, they'll assume it's still on."

"Let them assume. We don't have to tell them what's really going on."

She narrows her eyes at me. "Are you going to tell them that Kai is yours?"

"I hadn't really thought about it. It might be better if we leave that for a later conversation. For right now, I just want him to get to know his relatives and to be included in our family. You can't argue with that."

"I don't argue with it. I just said I was fine with it."

"Fine with it is definitely what you aren't. What's the matter? Why won't you talk to me? We can't keep doing this without communicating with each other."

"You want to communicate? You want to know what the matter is? Fine. I'll tell you. Maybe I'm just not as okay as I'm supposed to be with sharing Kai with someone else—or with several dozen other someone elses. Did that ever cross your mind? I've been alone with him for eight years and now you waltz into my life and all of a sudden I'm supposed to share him with you and the whole rest of your family. So I'm not as okay with that as I should be. So I might be really not okay with it at all. Is that what you want to hear?"

"So I should just back off and not be involved with him at all?" I fire back.

"That isn't what I said at all," she counters. "I never said that. Don't put words in my mouth."

"Did it ever cross your mind that it might really hurt to know that you had eight years alone with him while I was cruising around with no purpose in life and thinking Helena took my will to live when she left me? Did that ever occur to you? Did you ever stop to think I might resent you for having those years with him when I didn't get to? Did you ever think I might want to really hurt someone to make them hurt as much as I do that I didn't get to take care of him as a baby or help him learn how to walk or carry him around on my shoulders or teach him how to rock climb? Did you ever think of any of that? Did you ever think I might not be as okay with all this as I should be? Is that what you want to hear?"

She stares at me in blank shock. I break off breathing hard. My chest hurts from the tension of spitting all that out. I never planned to tell her that much and now I'm not sure if I broke something irreparable by saying it.

It hurts to have her look at me now that I actually said it. Now she knows she isn't the only one who might not be okay with all this.

She gapes at me for a second and then turns all the way away from me to stare out the window. I can't let her keep turning her back on me, but spinning her around and forcing her to face me isn't what's going to fix this.

I don't know what to say that *will* fix it. Maybe nothing will. I'm just about to walk away in defeat when I change my mind, go up behind her, and for no reason at all, I put my arms around her.

I just want to be near her. I want to know that everything's okay between us. I can't stand this vacuum of resentment and hostility holding us apart. I just want to make it go away so everything can be okay with us again.

She collapses against me so magically that I can't stand it. She barely whispers, "I'm sorry. I never did think of any of that. I'm sorry. I should have."

She feels so good in my arms and this ache in my heart hurts so much that I need to hold her tighter. I press my face into her hair and that smell detonates in my brain. I need more than this.... this businesslike arrangement. I need her. I need all of her.

"We both want what's best for him," I breathe. "The best thing for him is for us to be together—not just living together, but being a real couple."

She stiffens, but she doesn't pull out of my arms. She feels so alive and warm. That feeling sweeps me back to the night I spent with her in this room. It wakes all the old desires, including the desire to have something real with her. If we don't have it now, I want it. I want all of that and so much more.

All the times I've hugged her and kissed her on the head and wiped away her tears—what have those times been doing if not leading us to this?

I let my head fall on her shoulder and bury my face in her neck. She tenses all over, but it's the good kind of tension. She quivers with lightning racing up and down her skin under her clothes, and when I crawl my mouth higher toward her ear, she gasps and shudders.

I want to whisper so many things into her ear. I want to tell her that I love her. I want to joke and make her laugh. I want to tell her to strip for me and bend over so I can attack her in raving fury.

All those feelings struggle for dominance in my deepest being. I want it all with her, but she can barely stay in the same room with me. I can't say any of those things or she might run away from me.

This is too good to risk it and her body tells me all I need to know. I don't need to talk. My body speaks to her and her body answers in the same language. She can't hold back the rasp of her strained breath through her teeth and the blissful sigh of ecstasy when I rock her in my arms.

I want to tell her to give herself to me, but her body tells me that she already is. She doesn't stop me from nuzzling lower to the collar of her shirt. I want to tear her clothes and make her scream before Kai comes back, but taking it slow like this means so much more.

It might make her question, but it's enough just to hold her and feel that she feels the same way I do. I can live with that, right here in this moment.

She stands up and turns around much more slowly. She doesn't shove me away, but when she faces me, she keeps her eyes down. I want to make her look at me, but the next instant, she very slowly lifts her eyes to mine.

They burn with unimaginable sadness. I can't tell if she's sad for me or herself, but at least she's looking at me, and before I can decide what to do, she puts her arms around me and hugs me.

"Thank you," she chokes in my ear. "I don't know how to thank you for doing this for me. I've never been so grateful for anything ever. I'm sorry. I don't know how to act around you and I.... I didn't want to swallow my pride and thank you the way I should have. I thought....I thought.....I don't know what I thought, but thank you. I'm so grateful...."

She breaks off with another choking sound and my heart bleeds. Her arms and her body feel so unimaginably good. I'm holding her and everything's okay. I want....I don't want anything but this.

She leans back again, but it still takes all her effort to make eye contact. Unimaginable love overflows my heart for her. She's so important to me. I never want to lose her and now I know I never will. She'll always be in my life one way or another.

I don't know what to do or say next. We should talk about everything we're going to do with Kai, but I don't want to change the conversation this soon. I just want to stand here and be with her and feel how wonderful it is that everything's okay between us.

Without warning, she leans in and kisses me. She takes me so completely by surprise that I don't respond at first. I just stand there in shock and then I feel her lips. God Almighty, she feels incredible!

My arms migrate to her waist and I start kissing her back. Before I know what hit me, we're kissing like anything. My brain can't keep up with what's happening. Is our relationship changing?

I can't tell. I only know I'm kissing her and this thing is skyrocketing off the charts in the biggest possible way. She presses her body against me and my body answers her in that same wordless language.

I start to get hard and she grinds her delectable box on my knob to drive me out of this world. My hand slides down to her ass and she moans in delirious passion when I crush her into me.

Her breasts compress against my chest and I have to squeeze them. I have to touch all of her and feel her melting and squirming and undulating into me just as ravenously. Oh, hell yes.

Her hair tumbles over my face and envelops me in her scent. I dissolve in her kiss and it lights up my body as never before. We both stagger toward the bed tugging and squeezing and touching everything at once.

Her hands dart under my shirt and her touch makes me gasp in ragged agony. She slides down to my belt and then to my ass. She pulls me into her harder. She wants it bad—almost as badly as I do.

We land on the mattress and we both go to town on each other's clothes. She strips my shirt over my head, but when I try to get her pants off, she dives in and kisses my stomach.

I spasm at the first scorching kiss on my sides, and when she won't stop, I collapse groaning on the bed. She works up and down my stomach and chest until she comes to my belt.

She tugs it loose and inches lower. She drags her cruel teeth over my bulge and teases my shaft through my pants. Holy fuck, I want her so bad!

I yank her shirt out of her waistband and she lets me pull it over her head while she jerks my belt off. She keeps burying her face in my crotch, but I don't want to just lie here while she does that. I want to touch her and feel her and join my body with hers.

I pull her toward me to kiss her again and she climbs on top of me to straddle me. We've been here before, but that isn't what I want, either.

I let her ride me while she takes off her bra. I play with her breasts for a minute, but she doesn't respond—not the way I want her to.

I grab her and turn her over onto her back. She wraps her legs around me when I kiss her and I lie down between her legs, but our pants still get in the way.

I rise on my knees and her haunted eyes drill into me from below. She breathes deeply and sways under my hand when I touch her. She doesn't look away and she lets me see how much she wants this.

I start unbuttoning her pants and I make sure she stays with me when I slide them down along with her panties. I want her more than anything, but I need to know she's with me before anything else. I can't let her drift off somewhere else.

I throw her pants on the floor, and when I look deep into her eyes, she doesn't try to hide her volcanic desire from me. She arches her back for me and undulates her breasts and stomach and hips when I stroke her beautiful skin.

She spreads her legs and her lips quiver when I start touching her. She shows me her face contorting in desire and she moans openly when I get near her dripping flesh. She tries to twist onto my fingers and she grabs my wrist trying to pull me in. She really does want it.

She rears off the bed without breaking eye contact and she grabs me between my legs trying to drag me closer. "Please...." she husks. "Please....please take me....I need you so bad......"

She starts working on my fly. I don't stop her. I sit back and watch her pop the button and slide down my zipper. She peels my pants open, slides her hand down inside my shorts, and starts stroking me with long, expert caresses.

I can't move. I sit back and watch her eyes as she teases me to raging hardness. She doesn't stop. I want to make her show me how much she wants me. I want her to show me how much she needs me to take her.

I love watching her like this. I love seeing her surrender to all the devouring lust in her. She's so fucking passionate and the conflicting emotions displayed in her eyes and face make her mind-blowingly beautiful.

Her hand burns my skin so bad I can hardly take it, but watching her electrifies me so much that I just have to sit here and savor the moment.

She pulls me out and slowly slides my pants down so she holds me in her bare, hot hand. She bends down and I gasp when she takes me in her mouth. Oh, my living God, she's good!

My every muscle and nerve tenses when she starts sucking. Her mouth milks me to such a throbbing hardness that it hurts. I need her. I need her all the way before I explode right here, but some part of me can't move to stop her.

This feeling, this feeling that she's showing me how much she needs me—I need to keep feeling this as long as possible. I need to feel that she has to have me, that she'll do anything to have me. This feeling does something to me that not even her body can give me.

Her hands travel over my chest and stomach while she sucks me. She caresses me so lovingly. I could sit here all day and enjoy this, but it doesn't work that way.

I push her off roughly and make her topple backward onto the bed. She falls on her back and the drunken ecstasy written all over her face is more than I can stand. She writhes in front of me all beautiful and glowing and naked. She spreads her legs and pushes her breasts up where I can massage them.

She moans and whines and sobs in need when I pinch her nipples and finger her slit. I can't get enough of seeing how insatiably hot she is.

Plenty of women have shown me their desire before, but none of them has ever resisted me as much as she has. None of them ever resisted me at all.

Her behavior now means so much more because she's worked so hard to suppress and avoid it. She didn't want to come to this place with me, but now that she's here, she doesn't try to hide it anymore. She wants me. She needs me. She needs me as much as I need her.

I start to lean forward when I hear the apartment door open downstairs. "I'm home, Mom!" Kai yells up the stairs.

"Okay, sweetie!" she calls.

Her eyes flick over to me and we both freeze. Are we going to stop, now that Kai is here?

She doesn't move to get up. She doesn't change her position at all. She still lies before me, naked and magnificent.

I get up, cross the room, and shut the door quietly before I go back over to the bed. I'm still raging hard and she still lies sprawled before me with her legs apart.

I drop onto my hands and knees above her. I want to kiss her, but it's too important that I keep looking into her eyes. I need to stay connected with her while we do this.

She doesn't shrink even once. She raises her arms to touch me and she extends her legs to draw me in. She holds my gaze all the way down, down, down.

My weight sinks into her. Her lips shiver and she winces in the most delightful possible way when my stiff rod glides into her wetness. Oh, my God, she feels amazing!

She collapses back with her eyes blazing as I set up a steady rhythm. Her body matches mine exactly. She never breaks that cadence and her whining cries set my brain on fire.

I can't help but speed up and she moans a little louder, but not loudly enough for Kai to hear. I feel myself escalating and pounding her up the bed. She bursts into madness and drives herself down on my thrusts until our bodies smash together in a quick, hot explosion that leaves us both breathless.

She holds my eyes all the way until the end, but just when I think I can't take it anymore, she buries her mouth in my chest the way she did that first night. She muffles her torrential screams in my skin and her muscles clench around me in such a tight, burning fist that I explode into her.

I want to scream and roar and bellow at her, but I can't do that with Kai around. I cover my mouth in her hair and a colossal tide of emotion grips me as I release into her. I don't want this to end, but I know it will.

As soon as we finish, she has to get up and go start making dinner. One of us needs to get out of this bedroom quickly so Kai doesn't start to wonder where we are.

She tilts back, but instead of falling onto the bed, she lunges farther up and starts kissing me like anything. She devours my mouth even more wildly than before if that's even possible.

She doesn't stop kissing me when she squirms out from under me, stands up, and starts moving over to where she dropped her clothes. I follow her trying to grasp every single second of contact with her lips.

Her eyes glisten just beyond my nose. She won't stop kissing me when she bends down and picks up her pants. She giggles while she straightens them out and starts pulling on her panties.

I chuckle into her mouth. We're goofing around again and the big joke is that we don't stop kissing even as she's getting dressed to leave the room.

Something crashes down the hall in Kai's room and she breaks off. She snickers while she quickly kicks her legs into her pants, snatches her shirt off the floor, and pulls it over her head before she dashes out of the room carrying her bra in one hand.

She leaves me sitting there naked with our combined juices still coating my shaft. I want her back here. I want to taste her sweet fruit in my mouth while I tease her to oblivion, but that will have to wait.

I hear her talking to Kai down the hall.

"Where's Jayden, Mom?" he asks.

"I don't know, sweetie," she replies. "He's around here some-where."

"Did you talk to him about the horse trekking trip?"

"Yeah, I talked to him about it."

"So can I go?" he asks.

"I already said yes, sweetheart. You don't have to keep asking."

He hesitates. "Are you okay, Mom?"

"I'm fine, sweetie. I have to go downstairs and start dinner."

She walks off and I can't help smirking, but I need to get dressed and get out of this room before he comes looking for me.

I take my clothes, hide behind the door while I get dressed, and then wait for him to go downstairs before I duck into my room.

This is definitely another first. I've never hidden from a woman's child before to cover up the fact that we just had sex. My whole life is taking a turn for the surreal.

Chapter 18: Quinn

Kai squints across the grounds toward the Aldrich Estates. "Are we really going back in there?"

"Don't worry," I tell him. "It won't be like last time. It's just a house like any other except that it's bigger."

"A whole lot bigger," he murmurs and his eyes skim across the mansion's enormous walls and grand roofs.

"You can believe your mom," Jayden chimes in. "She used to run up and down the halls in her socks and slide on the tiles until she banged into the walls. She used to get in trouble for sliding down banisters and tracking mud all over the carpets. She never treated it like anything but a normal house."

"Don't tell him that!" I counter. "Don't listen to him, sweetie. Don't slide down the banisters or run around in your socks."

Jayden laughs. "You loved it and you would love to do it now. Admit it. We all know you've been dying to do it ever since you 'grew up'." He puts air quotes around the last words and then smirks.

I bite back the urge to join in the joke. "We're still guests here and we still have to behave ourselves."

"No way." Jayden turns to Kai. "Enjoy yourself. Simon and Andrea sure do. You go off with them. They'll get you into plenty of trouble and I can promise you they won't get you to do anything your mom hasn't already done."

Kai looks back and forth between us and a grin creeps over his face. "Really?"

"Really. If she tries to convince you that she was all virtuous back then, you come and talk to me and I'll tell you all about it. Your mom was the biggest troublemaker on the block back then."

"I was not a troublemaker," I mutter. "I was just a normal kid."

Kai snorts with laughter. "Will you tell me if she *doesn't* try to convince me that she was virtuous?"

"I might. Now come on. Let's go see what's up."

The three of us head up the driveway. Merrick and the other butlers aren't here to greet us and the three of us wear casual clothes. We aren't here for a dinner party or any other fancy occasion. We're just here so Kai can get to know his cousins and the rest of his relatives.

We only make it halfway to the house before two kids burst through the giant front doors. They yell and wave and laugh. Their voices echo over the estate and they take off running toward us.

Jayden gives Kai a shove. "Go on. Get out of here."

Kai breaks into a run, meets up with the boy and girl, and they exchange a few words before they run off somewhere else. Their voices get farther away and eventually fade into the grounds.

"There you go," Jayden murmurs. "That's all there is to it."

"Could you not encourage him to misbehave? He still has to learn how to make a good impression on strangers."

"I'm not encouraging him to misbehave. I'm encouraging him to be a normal kid. You said you weren't a troublemaker. You were just a normal kid and you said you wanted him to grow up normally. He can grow up normally here. You're living proof of that."

He glances over and meets my gaze for a second before I break eye contact and look away. I've been trying a lot harder to look him in the eye ever since we did it in my bedroom.... again.

I know I need to get used to looking him in the eye, but I still find it incredibly hard. I keep seeing that look in his eye, the look that tells me he's thinking about doing it again. He looks at me all the time now and holding that look doesn't get any easier.

In fact, it only gets harder because now I really want it, too. I can't stop thinking about it, but I know I shouldn't go there.

I can't bring myself to wish I didn't do it. I enjoyed it and I'm not so stupid as to think I won't do it again. I'm certain I will, but I can't help wishing that I wouldn't. Doing it with Jayden only complicates things more than they already are.

He keeps mentioning that the best thing for Kai is for us to be a real couple. I know he's right, but I still can't overcome my resistance.

I can think of a thousand reasons not to. Jayden is a friend. I know that now. He has to be a friend if he agreed to this arrangement just so I can continue to have a relationship with Kai.

I don't want to mess that up, but doing it with Jayden isn't helping anything. I don't seem able to separate our friendship from doing the right thing for Kai from wanting Jayden.

I want him. I can't deny that anymore. I want him a hell of a lot more than I'm able to show him I want him. I can't stop myself from fantasizing about doing it with him again.

I've spent the last several years hearing every woman in town talk about how hot he is. I knew intellectually that he was attractive, but his magnetic nature makes it so much more obvious, now that we're actually doing it on a regular basis.

He can make melt with a look. He can make me wet just by passing me in the kitchen at breakfast. Being in the same room with him makes me breathless like I might be about to collapse in a puddle of lust. I've never responded to any man like this. I don't know how to handle it or even if I can handle it.

He seems to respond to me the same way. He constantly comes up to me at random times when Kai isn't around. He doesn't seem to be able to keep his hands off me, and when he touches me, he always winds up escalating as far as possible before Kai interrupts us.

Jayden keeps ambushing me in the laundry room, in his room, in the kitchen, at my desk, in the bathroom....anytime he can get near me when Kai isn't around.

All Jayden has to do is walk into the same room with me and it's all on. I don't know what's happening, but I don't want it to stop. I just wish I knew what it meant and where it was going.

He slips his hand into mine as we get closer to the entrance. "Are you ready for this?"

"Sure. Why not?"

He pauses at the base of the steps and turns to me. I can never look away from his eyes when he looks at me like that. My breath catches as a wave of desire hits me. He glances down at my mouth and gives me one quick kiss on the lips before he turns away.

We go inside, but we don't go to the big hall. We go through the foyer to the back terrace bathed in sunshine where Mrs. Aldrich, Stuart, Eva, Pauline, and her husband Reggie lounge around on the deck furniture.

Stuart comes toward us, shakes Jayden's hand, and then hugs him. "Hey, man! The kids are running around here somewhere. Where's your boy?"

"He found them already. They ran off together."

"That's good." Stuart turns to me and holds out his arms to hug me. "It's great to see you again, Quinn."

"Thanks, Stuart. You, too."

We go through all the usual greetings. I've known these people all my life, but it still feels weird being here. They think Jayden and I are going to get married and they don't know about Kai being Jayden's son.

None of these people know anything about the whole motion to vacate fiasco, either. They don't know the nightmare I've been going through for the past few weeks, but it's a comfort to know this whole thing has been just as big a nightmare for Jayden. I really was selfish not to realize what this must have done to him.

Things have gotten a lot easier now that we both know where we stand. It's just the constant sex that keeps muddling things up.

I have to steel myself for the inevitable when it comes to greeting Mrs. Aldrich. "Darling!" she exclaims. "You look magnificent. You look even better like this than you did at dinner the other night."

"Thanks, Mrs. Aldrich. You look great, too."

"Oh, don't try to flatter me! You looked outstanding in that dress, but now you look more like the little girl I used to know. You were so charming then! You still are. Come over and sit down by me. I want to talk to you about absolutely everything!"

She drags me toward a picnic table under a large green canvas umbrella. I can just imagine what she wants to talk to me about.

Jayden stays where he is and I hear him talking to Stuart about the horse trekking trip they want to take the kids on. I still haven't made up my mind if I want to go. I mean, of course I want to go, but I don't know if I should.

The trip is supposed to be a chance for Kai and Jayden to bond with Jayden's relatives. Me being there might be a distraction from that and how would it work if Jayden keeps springing all this sex on me?

Mrs. Aldrich sits down on a rattan divan under the umbrella and waves to an Adirondack chair nearby for me to take a seat. Then she leans over and pats my arm.

"I know Jayden moving in with you was just a temporary convenience, but we both know it can't last. Now, we have Weeping Willow Lodge in Waterford. You'd be much more comfortable there, don't you think? You'd have more space and Jayden wouldn't have to throw his money away paying all that rent. The cabin isn't all it's cracked up to be, but the estate would be happy to renovate it for you to bring it up to date. It could be another temporary solution until you and Jayden take over the estate with the rest of his grandfather's legacy."

I stare at her in shock. Weeping Willow Lodge is so much more than a cabin. It's almost as big as Aldrich Estates and just as grand.

I can't imagine ever living there, but if the Aldrich family still expects us to get married, we might have to--we might have to move there, not get married. We aren't getting married.

I don't tell her that paying my own rent is a matter of personal pride and integrity for me. I also don't tell her that Jayden hasn't given me a cent toward rent or food since he moved in with me and Kai. Jayden hasn't offered and I haven't asked. We don't discuss money—ever.

I would never tell her that and there is no way in hell that I would ever take a penny of his money. Like hell I will.

Her last comment is the one that really slaps me in the face. Jayden didn't tell me that Aldrich Estates was included in his grandfather's legacy. Whoever he marries will be living here.

That's all the more reason I can't marry him. I could never live here. I don't think I could even live at Weeping Willow Lodge. It's way too fancy and I like my life exactly the way it is. I don't want to change anything and I don't want a bigger house. I especially don't want to live in a damn mansion or a castle like the estate.

Mrs. Aldrich throws up both hands and starts digging in her pocket for her phone. "Now, darling! Eva and Pauline and I have been discussing the decorations for the wedding. We understand you want to use your own dressmaker, but we should at least discuss the design and the color and everything so we can coordinate with the florist and the decorator and the cakemaker so everything matches. Now, darling! Which dress designer do you plan to use?"

I open my mouth to answer, but no sound comes out. I haven't even agreed to this wedding yet. I'm not even sure I could afford to get a dress specially designed and made for me. All of that is so far out of my wheelhouse that I can't even force myself to think about it.

Mrs. Aldrich doesn't seem to notice, nor does she notice that I didn't answer her question. She rises out of her divan, waves, and calls across the terrace. "Pauline! Come over here. We need to talk about the arrangements for the wedding."

I glance over and see for the first time that Jayden, Stuart, and Reggie aren't here anymore. I'm all alone with Mrs. Aldrich and her daughters.

The two sisters come over and sit down at the table. Pauline pulls out her phone and starts flipping through images in her photo gallery while she bombards me with questions, ideas, and suggestions.

"I love this cake design, don't you? We could decide on the cake design and then show it to the florist so they replicate the flowers from the cake. We'll need to bring in the decorators and plan the decorations for the marquee and the floral arch and the carpet of rose petals that you're going to walk down. We'll need to coordinate with everyone on your side of the family so your parents and anyone else in your party matches the color scheme. Do you know what you're doing for the bridesmaids' dresses? We'll need to know all that before we contract the decorators."

I stare down at her phone, too stunned even to blink. This wedding is turning into such a gigantic event. I want to run away and hide until it's all over, but I won't be able to do that if I'm the bride.

Pauline flips through images so fast that they start to blur. My brain shuts down trying to take it all in. I can't speak at all, much less tell these people that I won't be marrying Jayden at all. I couldn't face the catastrophe of dealing with their reactions.

"Who do you think you'll have for your bridesmaids, darling?" Mrs. Aldrich asks.

At that moment, a heavy hand comes to rest on my shoulder. I jump a foot in the air when Jayden's voice startles me out of my trance. "Excuse me, Mama. I hate to interrupt, but I need to borrow Quinn for a minute."

I scramble away from the table and he takes my hand on our way down the terrace. I have no idea where we're going or what he wants to talk to me about. It looks like we're heading out into the grounds, but the next second, he turns around the end of the house and enters through a side door.

Shadows close around us as he continues up the hall. We're in the back corner of the house behind the library.

He pulls me to a stop in the dark hall. "Are you okay? Sorry I didn't get there sooner."

"This can't continue," I tell him. "You have to tell them we aren't getting married."

"We aren't?" He cocks his head to study me. "So have you definitely made up your mind about that?"

"How can you even ask that? We aren't getting married."

"Why not? I thought we were getting along pretty well these last few days."

"Getting along! Is that what you call having all this sex?"

"Well, that and the fact that we're living together and raising a son together. What else is there but to get married?"

"We aren't getting married, Jayden," I tell him. "When are you going to drop the charade?"

"I don't want to drop it. I still don't understand why you don't want to get married. We have all the elements in place."

"For a start, we aren't in love and I'm not marrying a man I'm not in love with. Okay, so the sex is good, but...."

"Good!" he repeats. "Is that all it is?"

"That isn't what I mean. We aren't even in a relationship. We're friends and parents and we have a lot of sex. That isn't a relationship and it definitely isn't a relationship good enough to build a marriage on."

"What would be? What would you add to make it good enough to build a marriage on?"

"Just what I said. We would have to be in a relationship and be in love and actually want to share our lives with each other. We wouldn't just be shacked up for a legal convenience."

"I've said it before," he replies. "It would be better for Kai if we were in a real relationship."

"It might be better for Kai if we were, but the fact remains that we aren't. We aren't in a real relationship and we aren't a couple. I can't believe you would let your family go to such lengths to plan out our wedding without telling them the truth. Your mother...."

I break off. I can't tell him about her offer for us to move into Weeping Willow Lodge. I'm not ready for that.

He scrutinizes me for a long time—too long. All at once, he raises his hand, rests it against my cheek, and kisses me, but he doesn't attack me to tear my clothes off and plow into me the way he usually does.

He kisses me slowly with his eyes burning into me from inches away. His lips swirl with mine while his eyes hold me in that delirious hypnotic dimension I don't understand. It just makes me throb for him.

He finally eases off just enough to whisper under his breath, but his lips don't break contact with mine. "I want to, Quinn. I want to fall madly in love with you and love you for the rest of my life. I want us to be a real couple and get married and live happily ever after. I want us to do it for real."

"But you don't," I reply in the same low undertone. "You aren't madly in love with me and I'm not madly in love with you. We love each other as friends. We care about each other and admire each other as friends. We wouldn't live happily ever after if we got married because we don't feel that way about each other."

He kisses me for another long, slow, silent minute. "You're right. I don't feel that way about you. I just want you."

He lays his hand on my back and drives his hard prick into me. That feeling of his hips flexing to pump into me makes me moan in agony. He watches my eyes drift out of focus and my lips quiver apart in a sob of endless pleasure. I want him, too. I want him all the way.

"You want that, don't you?" he growls. "That turns you on, doesn't it?"

I yelp as he grabs my breast with his other hand and pumps in one more time. "Yes!" I sob. "I need you!"

He glances around and then marches me backward without releasing his hold on me. He pushes me into the library, kicks the door shut, and shoves me back it. He crams his pelvis between my legs and keeps driving his hips between my legs until I moan for him.

"Say it's more than good," he snarls under his breath. "Say this is the best you ever had. Say I'm the best you ever had. Say you can't live without me. Say you need me right *there*."

He drills in even harder and I have to suppress a scream when he splits my legs apart. I grasp at his shoulders, and in a lightning move of ultimate mastery, he slams my wrist back against the door.

I squeal in deepest desire as he cracks my thighs apart. I feel myself rising on a wave of passion that sweeps me away every time he does this to me.

He rears back and holds my gaze with unstoppable power while he starts unbuttoning my pants. "Say it," he rasps. "Say it's more than good. Say it's the best you ever had."

"Yes!" I gasp. I can't stop shaking, I want him so bad. He knows he's the best I ever had. He knows he's the best there is and he holds me in the palm of his hand.

"Say you can't live without me."

"Jayden...." I begin, but at that moment, he rips my pants open and crams his hand down inside my panties. His fingers vanish into my saturated tissues and I end up screaming at the mind-blowing intensity.

He shoves his fingers all the way in and I can't stop myself from bucking my hips down on his hand.

"Say you can't live without me," he demands. "Say it, Quinn. You know you need me. You can't live without this, can you? You would come begging for it if I decided not to take you."

I can't look away from those all-seeing eyes. I hear myself screaming as the devouring desire for him breaks all bounds and I spike into a crushing orgasm that rocks me to my core.

He dives in and kisses me for a second before he leans back and watches me. "You can't live without me, Quinn. You need this so bad.

You can't get enough of this. You could never go back to living without this. You're mine. You're all mine. Your body is mine. You can't stop yourself from giving yourself to me."

His voice and his words and his flinty hard eyes destroy my last resistance. "Yes! I need you!"

"Say you're mine. Say it, Quinn. I won't take you until you say it."

I whimper in defeat. He knows it's true. He can command me with his eyes. He knows I would never be able to resist him. He's too good and my body already needs him too badly.

He rips his hand out of my panties and pushes my pants down to my knees. He drops on one knee in front of me and buries his face between my legs.

I sob in agony as he drives me back to the brink of insanity. I'm already shaking all over from the first orgasm. I don't know if I can survive another one, but he doesn't show any signs of slowing down.

He mauls me with his lips and tongue, and when I move my hands over to his hair, he grabs my wrists and wrestles them behind my back. He pins them in one hand and grabs my ass in the other.

He pulls me into his mouth with a crushing grip while he devours me in greedy bites. He growls under his breath in animal satisfaction while he feasts his heart out on my swollen, twitching flesh.

I can't take this. I need him so fucking bad, and when he lets go of my ass to slide his fingers inside me, I can't hold back. I collapse against the door whining and crying as another catastrophic climax takes me away to the limits of sanity.

I struggle and thrash against his cruel hold, but he fixes me in place with his masterful mouth until it's all over.

My knees buckle the instant he backs off. He stands up and catches me as I fall against his chest. I can't see as the last tortured convulsions rock my body.

He wraps his arms around me kissing my neck and ear, but each of those kisses only makes me quiver and moan even more than I already am.

"Please.... Jayden......" I gasp. "I.....can't....."

"Shhhh," he whispers in my ear. "Never mind."

"I.... can't......" I don't know what I'm trying to say, but I have to say something.

"That's all right," he breathes. "You don't have to."

"I....can't......Jayden.......I can't......live without you....."

I break down moaning and whining on his shoulder. I want to cry, but this ravenous desire for him won't let me. Pleasure still pulsates through my body. I've never experienced anything like this before.

I know I need him. I could never go back to the way it was before. I know that now. I just don't know how to cross that last barrier holding us apart. I'm not sure if anything can cross it, but I know I'm his now. My body is all his. My mind just hasn't caught up with the rest of me yet.

"Baby!" he whispers in my ear. "You are so precious to me!"

He strokes my hair and the back of my neck, but he doesn't take it any further. After a few minutes, he pulls my pants up, zips them, and buttons the button.

Did my confession finally push him away? Is that all he wanted—to know that he had me? Maybe he'll lose interest in me, now that he knows he conquered me. Was that the only reason he was interested in me—because I resisted him?

He waits until I get myself together, and when he kisses me, his eyes leave me in no doubt that he can reduce me to a quivering wreck whenever he wants. I really can't resist him anymore. I'm his and he knows it.

He takes a step back and levels me with the same penetrating stare. "Are you okay? Are you ready to go back out there?"

I nod and gulp. I can't say anything. I want to hide in his arms. I feel like I'm about to fall apart if he turns his back on me.

He takes my hand and leads me back out onto the grounds. He doesn't let go of me, which is good because I couldn't function on my own right now.

We go back to the terrace where Merrick is serving lunch to Mrs. Aldrich and the others. The three kids sit off to one side eating sandwiches and talking. They finish early and rush away into the grounds.

I don't have to wonder what they're doing out there. Jayden and I did the same thing when we were their age. I guess he's right. Kai can have a normal childhood here as easily as anywhere else.

Is it possible he could grow up normally at Weeping Willow Lodge.... or here? Jayden grew up here and he's as normal as they come. Eva and Pauline aren't too snobbish, either. In fact, they aren't snobbish at all.

None of the Aldrichs have ever treated me differently because I didn't have their money. My parents were working class, but none of Jayden's family ever seemed to care that I came from a completely different social class. Everything about my time here at the estate was normal. Maybe I'm making too big a deal about that.

Jayden and I sit down and have lunch with the others. Jayden stays near me for the rest of the visit, and if his mother or his sisters ever mention the wedding, he deflects it by saying that we'll work it all out in time.

"Everything depends on setting the date, darling," Mrs. Aldrich tells him. "We can't do anything until we know that."

"I understand, Mama," he replies. "Quinn and I will discuss it and we'll let you know when we decide."

Chapter 19: Jayden

I walk into Quinn's apartment and see her just getting up from her desk. I shouldn't call it Quinn's apartment. It's my apartment now, too, even though I'm still not paying rent. She never mentions money. She doesn't even mention me contributing toward her food bill even though she feeds me three meals a day.

She even goes as far as packing me lunch every day. She doesn't give me a *Star Wars* lunchbox like she gives Kai, but her making my lunch makes it just as good as if she did give me a lunchbox.

She puts it in a plain plastic kitchen container and she always gives me a pastrami sandwich. Pastrami is my favorite as well she knows.

She always had pastrami sandwiches in her lunch when we were growing up. The Aldrich Estates housekeeper at the time always packed me packaged snacks for lunch and Quinn and I always swapped so I could eat her sandwich.

It means a lot that she remembers and gives me the same thing now. All the money in the world can't make up for that and she's always doing little things like that for me. I don't want to read too much into it, but it sure does make me wonder if it means something more. I wish it did.

She gets up from her desk and smiles at me. "Hey! You're home early."

I pull out the container and hold it up before I put it on the counter. "I really appreciate you doing this for me."

"Sure. A man has to eat."

"You don't have to, but it means a lot that you do it."

She comes over to the counter, opens the container, and puts it in the dishwasher. She starts moving around the kitchen getting ready for Kai to come home from school.

I watch her going through her routine. She makes my being here routine, too. She just makes my lunch at the same time that she makes Kai's. She treats me being here like it's normal now.... almost like we're already married.

"Listen, Quinn," I begin. "We need to talk about this whole marriage thing."

"Why do we have to?" she asks over her shoulder. "I thought we already discussed that."

"We discussed it, but we didn't come to any definite conclusion. We can't keep doing this without making a decision one way or the other. We can't keep living together platonically for the next ten years until Kai leaves home."

"Why can't we?" she asks.

"First of all, because you aren't legally his parent anymore and I'm supposed to get married so I can inherit my grandfather's estate."

She spins around in a heartbeat. I finally have her attention.

"Even if I didn't have to get married to inherit the estate, I want to. I want Kai to grow up in a two-parent home which means marrying someone. I want more kids and I want them to grow up in a two-parent home, too. I don't want to be single anymore, and if you're absolutely set that you won't marry me, that means me moving out."

She doesn't say a word, but her eyes tell me she knows exactly what that means. She gulps.

I need to relieve the tension somehow, and if I go near her, we'll probably wind up doing it again. I sit down at the counter instead. We need to discuss this like adults without tearing each other's clothes off.

"Marrying you solves all those problems. I want to share Kai with you and getting married is the perfect solution to that. I want to marry you. You're the only woman I want to marry. You keep saying we don't have a relationship, but I want that. I want us to start building a relationship and falling in love with each other for real like you say so we can live happily ever after."

She lowers her eyes once and then meets my gaze. "I want that, too. I just don't know how."

My eyebrows fly up. "You do? When did you decide that?"

She shrugs. "I don't know. I guess it's been coming for a while now. I just...." Her face convulses. "It scares the shit out of me."

"Me, too, baby." I hold out my hand and she crosses to the other side of the counter. She takes my hand, but we both keep the counter between us. We're both safer that way.

The elevator dings and she takes her hand back before Kai barges in. He doesn't notice anything because nothing is happening.

He dumps his backpack on the counter next to Quinn and goes over to the fridge. "Mom! That boy Tom just showed up in my class today! He wants to meet up at the park this weekend. Can we go?"

"You're going to Will's sleepover at the lake so we won't be going to the park."

"Oh, yeah!" he exclaims. "I forgot all about that."

"Go upstairs, get out of your school clothes, and start getting your stuff together. I'm taking you over to Will's in an hour."

He races off upstairs. Quinn shoots me a smile that warms my heart. She's Kai's mother and I'm his father. This must be the kind of understanding smile of silent communication that fathers and mothers have shared for all of human history when their kids do something childlike.

I want to keep sharing those moments with her. I want her to feel this warmth in her heart when she looks at me—her child's father. I want to see her pregnant with my children and watch her give birth and raise those kids from day one. I don't want to wait around anymore.

Is that what falling in love is? Do I feel that way because she's my friend.... or because she's my future? I don't even know what falling in love is if it isn't that. I don't know where friendship ends and love begins.

She gets busy making dinner. She goes through the usual routine of taking stuff out of the fridge even though Kai won't be here. It will just be the two of us....alone....for the first time.

"Hey," I murmur across the counter. "Let's go out to dinner tonight, just you and me."

She jumps a foot in the air and looks up at me in terror. "Really?"

"Yeah. Come on. We have the house to ourselves tonight. Let's go out. We can make this our first date."

She blinks at me and then bursts out in nervous laughter. "A date? Seriously?"

"Why not? We're supposed to be getting into a relationship."

"You mean we won't stay locked in here doing it all night?"

"We can do that later—after dinner."

She breaks down laughing again and starts putting everything back in the fridge. "All right. If I have to."

"You don't have to. You can go out with another guy if you really want to."

She beams at me and she looks genuinely happy about this. "I don't want to go out with another guy."

That look in her eyes makes me really want to attack her, but not tonight. We both need to learn to control ourselves if we're going to make this real. We already know the chemistry is there. We need everything else that goes with a relationship.

"Can I ask you a question?" I ask.

"Go ahead."

"You and Max.... how did it work out with you two? How did you meet and how did you get involved?"

"What do you want to know that for?" she asks. "What does Max have to do with you and me?"

"I don't really have any experience with actual dating. I thought I was in love with Helena and look how that turned out. I guess I don't really trust myself to do it the way it should be done. I don't really understand the process. I thought you might know better since you and Max were so.... well, I don't even know what being in love is, but you two obviously were. You know better than I do."

She keeps working around the kitchen so she doesn't have to look at me. "I don't think my experience with Max will help me out much with you."

"Why not?" I ask.

"Because you're so different from him....and because I'm so different with you than I was with him. I'm a completely different person. I'm a mother....and I'm different with you. I could never do with him what I do with you."

"Do you mean you didn't have a good sex life with him?"

She blushes, but she doesn't avoid the subject. "We had a good sex life before he got sick, but it wasn't like this. It was.... sweeter. It wasn't as.....how do I say this....?"

I wait, but she doesn't answer. "It wasn't what?"

She turns bright red and waves her hands. "It wasn't as....shall we say......It wasn't as physical. Sex with him was less physical. I didn't react to him the way I react to you. It was slower and calmer and more about the emotionality. It wasn't nearly so...."

"What?" I ask again. "Tell me. If there's something wrong with it...."

"There's nothing wrong with it. It's just.... hot. I guess that's the only word for it. Sex with him was nothing like this."

A rush of adrenaline twists through my guts. Sex with her is hot as fuck. I can't imagine having sex with any other woman. She eclipses everyone I've ever had. Even going near her makes me feel like her energy is burning me.

Every drop of her juices scorches my skin. Every glance from her blisters me beyond belief. She's by far the hottest woman I've ever laid eyes on.

The sight of her squirming and writhing under me when I touch her—the way she arches her back and spreads her legs and consumes my eyes yearning for me to take her—the way she claws her fingertips into my back—the way she grabs my ass to cram me down into her extra hard—I've never had sex like this in my life.

I'm not sure I can even stand it. In fact, I'm certain I can't. Is this what being in love means?

I swallow hard. It takes all my willpower to speak. "Are you saying we should back off and not do it anymore? Are you saying that's what it would take for us to have a real relationship? If you think that, I'll do it. Don't ask me how......"

"I don't think that's possible with us," she murmurs low. "I think we're passed the point of no return in that way. I'm just saying I don't think my experience with Max will do us much good in this situation. I wish I could tell you something useful, but I think we're breaking new territory here. We just have to figure it out for ourselves."

Kai comes back downstairs, opens his backpack, and starts pulling everything out of it. "What are you doing?!" Quinn exclaims. "Don't dump your stuff all over the kitchen floor! Take your gear upstairs, Kai!"

"I need to pack my stuff for the lake. Where's my sleeping bag, Mom?"

"Take your stuff upstairs, Kai! We aren't leaving until you put all your stuff away—and by away, I mean in your drawers and closet. Don't dump everything on the floor in your room, either."

"I don't have time for that!" He takes the empty backpack and rushes for the stairs. "I have too much else to do."

"Okay. We can spend a nice quiet evening at home, then."

"Mom!!" Kai hollers.

"It's your choice." She goes over to the couch, sits down, props up her feet, and opens a magazine. She pretends to read and completely ignores him.

He turns to me and his eyes tell me loud and clear that he wants to me intervene. "Don't look at me," I tell him. "You don't see me throwing my dirty socks on the floor."

He turns away and starts scrambling to pick up all his gear. He takes himself off upstairs and I chuckle until I see Quinn watching me with a strange expression on her face.

"What?" I ask.

"Nothing." She bends over her magazine and starts reading again.

Chapter 20:
Jayden

Quinn comes into the apartment and hangs her keys on the hook by the door. She turns around and her eyes mesmerize me with their power. "Alone at last."

I burst out laughing and she joins in. "Do you still want to go out to eat?" I ask.

"Well, I didn't make dinner. We'll need to eat something."

"Okay. Let's go."

"Uh.... Jayden?"

I turn around to face her. "Yeah?"

"Uh.....we need to talk about something."

"Okay. What is it?"

"If we're going to do this.... if we're going to get into a real relationship, like, for real....."

"Yeah?"

"Then we need to talk about.....money."

I relax. Of course we need to talk about money. I ease close to her and feel the unbreakable pull of her. I want to keep going until I touch her. "You know I'll always take care of you, Quinn. I would never let you go without. This is our first date so I'll pay and I'll drive us and everything...."

"That isn't what I mean."

"What do you mean? I make a lot more money than you do. It only makes sense for me to pay for everything."

"I mean, if we're really going to do this, then you would have to pay for *everything*. I mean, you wouldn't HAVE to, but...."

"Of course I would pay for everything. What else would I do?"

"I mean......you would pay for rent.... I mean, ALL of our rent and ....everything—power—food—internet—rent—taxes—everything."

"Yeah? What's wrong with that?"

She gulps and looks away for a second. She doesn't want to look at me, but she winds up doing it anyway. "Your mother....she suggested that we move into Weeping Willow Lodge. She said the estate would pay to renovate it and bring everything up to date and everything."

I nod. "Okay. We could do that."

"What I mean is......if we're really doing this...."

I deliberately stop myself from saying anything. She needs to get this out. It won't get any easier.

"If we got married, like, for real....then you would be the one to make those decisions about....where we live and everything....not me."

Now I see what she's getting at. Now I know why she found it so hard to say all that. "Is that what you want? Do you want me to make those decisions on behalf of all of us?"

She nods down at the floor and I can't keep away from her. I cross the last few feet of floor and put my arms around her. I want her more than ever now, but I want something so much more than just to tear her clothes off and make her scream in ways she's never been able to scream before because Kai was here.

I can't wait to see how she cuts loose now that he's gone. Just thinking about it makes my heart race, but this is more important.

I pull her over to the counter, sit down on a stool, and pull her between my knees. "Now I have a question for you, baby."

"What?" she asks.

"I want to know if you're on any kind of birth control."

Her eyes snap to my face and then she relaxes. She keeps her eyes down when she answers. "Max got prostate cancer. He had radiation to try to reduce the tumor and the doctors said it would affect his sperm. They told me to go on birth control so I wouldn't get pregnant with a baby that could have birth defects or congenital deformities or anything like that. I got an IUD and I've had it ever since. I had no reason to take it out."

I nod even though she isn't looking at me. I don't tell her that I want her to take it out so I can get her pregnant. That's a conversation for another day, but now I know what it will take when the time comes.

I kiss her on the forehead. "Thank you for telling me. Come on. Let's get changed and go out."

We go upstairs and split off to our separate rooms. I change my clothes, and when I finish, I hear her moving around in her bedroom.

I walk down the hall, but when I get near her door, I don't stop on the threshold the way I was planning to. I walk right in and sit down on the edge of the bed.

She's still slipping into a long, tight dress that hugs her curves all the way down to her knees. It makes her look just as stunning as she looked at Karina's wedding, except that Quinn is even more beautiful now because she's about to go out with me.

She blushes when she passes me on her way to her closet to put on her shoes. She catches me looking at her and her eyelashes dip. She looks so fucking hot that I feel myself starting to get hard.

I could so easily pull her down on the bed and take that dress off with my teeth, but that would defeat the purpose of going out on a date with her.

This is the first date I've ever been on—ever. Helena didn't date. We just kind of hooked up, moved in together, and then got married. I haven't dated anyone since.

I want to go out with Quinn. I want to make this official before we dive in with our boots on.

She puts on her heels and her hips sway so invitingly when she comes toward me. "I'm ready when you are," she tells me.

I stand up and take her hand to lead her out of the apartment. This feels.... real. I feel like we're in a relationship and maybe that we're already married. She follows me. She wants me to start making decisions on behalf of all three of us. What else does a relationship mean?

I want to take charge of her—of our whole family. That's what we are. We're family. She's my wife—or she will be soon.

Those words make me feel ten feet tall and bulletproof. My wife. My son. I'm a man now in a way I've never been before. I didn't even know what being a man was until tonight.

I lead her out to my car and open her door for her. She matches my movements exactly, and when we get to the restaurant and I hold out my hand to her, she takes it.

She blushes at me across the table. She is so incredibly beautiful. I really am the luckiest guy in the world and she's all mine. I know that now. The details will take care of themselves.

I find myself gazing down at her hand in mine. Something's missing. She should be wearing my ring on her finger to tell the whole world that she's mine. She should see it and feel it there while she works and does the dishes. I want her to see it and feel it and know that it means we're together forever.

We manage to get through the whole meal without talking about anything serious. What could be more serious than what we've already talked about and gone through?

Her eyes dart from side to side throughout the meal. "What are you looking at?" I finally ask. "Are you looking out for the guy you'd rather go out with?"

She blushes and laughs. Her eyes sparkle with....is she happy? Is she happy to be with me? "I keep looking around for Kai. I keep thinking I'm going to get in trouble for going out without him. I keep thinking he's home alone and the Police are going to come along and bust me for being out of the house this late at night."

"You might have to get used to it." I kiss her knuckles. "We should make this a regular thing."

"How would we do that? Who would take care of him if both of us went out?"

"I'm sure any number of people would be thrilled to take him off our hands. Simon and Andrea could invite him over for movie night.... or my mother could take him bowling....or....."

"Your mother.... bowls?" She explodes in laughter. "Cut it out!"

"You didn't know? She belongs to a ladies' league. She can be a terror. Don't ever bowl with her."

Quinn won't stop laughing. "You're pulling my leg!"

"Nope. You're going to learn all our family secrets. You're gonna wish you didn't."

She won't stop beaming at me. We're talking like friends again, but this means so much more now. We're getting married. She's going to be my wife. It's only a matter of time.

She follows my lead the same way when it's time to go home. We ride home in silence. We both know what's going to happen when we get back to the apartment, but maybe it's better if things don't run their natural course.

She wants me to take the lead, so it's my decision if they do. Would that be for the best? My decisions never made this much difference before or maybe I just didn't notice so much if they did.

Now it's up to me to make the right decision. I have to make the right decision. I have to do the right thing for her and Kai. This whole project depends on me.

The apartment looks different when we finally get home. I wander around the living room looking at everything. She wants me to decide where we live. She wants me to start taking the lead on all those decisions.

I can't make up my mind which would be better—staying here or moving to Weeping Willow Lodge. The lodge is nice. It's a lot more spacious and.... well, it's much nicer than this. It's more like Aldrich Estates.

This apartment, though—this apartment means something to all of us. It's home to all of us, including me. This apartment is home to me in ways nowhere else has ever been. I'm not sure anymore if I want to leave.

Would moving somewhere bigger and fancier benefit any of us at all? I can't think how except that it would make us seem richer. Quinn is right about that. It would be better for Kai and for Quinn and me if we stay here.

I hear her moving around upstairs. Is she changing out of her dress already?

I want to touch her and feel her and maybe do it with her while she's wearing that dress, but maybe that wasn't the point of going out on a date. Not doing it with her has once again become more important than doing it with her.

I go upstairs and waltz right into her bedroom. She still has the dress on. She takes her earrings off and kicks her heels into the closet. She looks so immaculately beautiful, mainly because she's so relaxed.

She's content here in her own bedroom. She isn't tense and defensive the way she was before. She really is okay with this decision. She's more than okay with it. She's happy with it and in it and about it. She's happy all about it.

"Are you okay?" she asks when she sees me watching her.

"I'm fine. I'm just thinking."

"About what?"

"About all of this—this whole project."

"Project?" She makes a face, but she's still smiling. "You make it sound like you're building a freeway or something."

I laugh. "I guess I am. That's one way of looking at it."

"So what are you thinking about it? How are the support girders coming along?"

"Well, I suppose the first thing we need to do is for me to move in here." I lean back on the bed and prop myself on my elbows. "I won't be sleeping in the guest room when we're married."

She freezes and her eyes go wide. She stares down at me with all her old horror and she gulps. "You....want to move in here?"

"Isn't that what being in a real relationship is? Isn't that what us getting married means? Would you rather move over to the guest room with me?"

"If you do that....if you move in here......that means Kai will know."

Now it's my turn to freeze. Of course it means Kai will know. The thought scares the shit out of me. It scares me as much as it obviously scares her, but that's the road we're on together.

She crosses the room and sits down next to me, but this ice-cold fear in my heart won't let me touch her or even look at her. This is the final frontier, the last barrier holding us apart. How would we tell Kai?

I find myself trembling at the thought of explaining to an eight-year-old boy that I'm going to move into his mother's bed. I've been doing it with her for days—weeks even.

This is a whole new level of terrifying. I almost feel like I should be asking his permission to marry his mother. I almost feel like he might beat me up for even suggesting it.

I could never touch her again if he doesn't approve. I could never have anything to do with her if he doesn't want me to.

I know he will. He'll be thrilled, but facing him still scares me to death. Nothing else about this scares me as much as this.

"What do you want to do about that?" she asks in a shaky undertone. She's as petrified of Kai as I am.

I shudder and shake it off. "We'll just have to work it out one way or the other. Anyway, we don't need to work it out tonight. He isn't here. We're alone. Let's just try to enjoy it before he comes home."

I say that, but I can't completely shrug off the pall that hangs over us. Kai will come home tomorrow and then....I don't know what will happen then.

She slumps and looks down at her hands. "Yeah," she breathes. "I guess you're right."

Neither of us can forget it, now that we're both thinking about it. I need to find a way to break the ice.

I turn to look at her, and when I do, she looks so beautiful and inviting that I put my arm around her shoulders and kiss her on the temple. "What would you like to do tonight?"

"What would *you* like to do tonight?"

"Why don't we just kick back and relax the way we used to? We could watch a movie or something."

She brightens up instantly. "Okay! That sounds good. I have some popcorn downstairs."

"Good. Let's change into our pajamas and I'll meet you in the living room."

She giggles, but right before we get up to go do it, she catches my eye and we both lean in to kiss each other. Kissing her feels wonderful. It doesn't feel so much like it will lead to sex even though that's still there. It will be waiting for us after we lay this foundation like she says.

We break apart at the same moment and I go into the guest room. I'll need to start taking my stuff into her room, so when I get out of my suit and put on my pajama pants and an old t-shirt, I take my suit into her room.

I lay it on the chair while she shimmies out of her dress. I find myself surveying her bedroom with the same appraising eye. Is there anything about this room that I want to change now that I'll be living in it?

I'll have to think about that and I don't need to do it tonight. Tonight is just for us.

She changes into a thick, fluffy bathrobe, puts on her slippers, and we both go downstairs. She puts the popcorn in the microwave and then brings a bag of chips, a package of cookies, and a bottle of juice over to the table.

I flop down in my usual place and kick my feet up on the coffee table. This feels fantastic. It feels like it used to only so much better. I could definitely spend the rest of my life like this.

She gets the popcorn out of the microwave and curls up next to me. She sits right next to me without trying to keep any space between us. "So what are we watching?" she asks.

"What is there?"

She picks up the remote, leans back on the cushions, and just be-cause, she scoots in next to me so she's leaning against me. I put my arm around her and she snuggles right into my side.

I kiss the side of her head while she switches on the TV and starts navigating around looking for something to watch. A rush of love grips me when I feel her weight against me. This is how it will be from now on, just the two of us together. It's perfect the way it is. It doesn't need to be anything else.

Chapter 21: Quinn

I slide into the booth and grin across the table at Harper, but my shoulders slump the instant I see her puffy face and bloodshot eyes. "What's wrong?"

"Ernesto dumped me! He said he was going to take me to Montenegro for Christmas and then he just dumped me! I can't believe it."

"Who's Ernesto?" I ask. "I never heard of him."

"I just met him on Wednesday and now it's over, just like that! What is wrong with all these guys? He's almost as bad as Jayden Aldrich."

I tense when she mentions Jayden. Harper doesn't know about me and Jayden. No one does. I'm not sure I have the courage to tell anyone, but I know I have to sooner or later.

I wouldn't bother to tell anyone if Jayden and I were just screwing around on the side, but this thing has gone way beyond that now. We're talking about getting married.

No, we *are* getting married. It's real. I know that now. Just don't ask me how I'm going to break the news to the rest of the world. Jayden and I have been telling them for years that we're just friends. Now we have to change all that and not as an act. It's for real.

The way I feel about him is definitely real. He's becoming the man in my life and I never would have believed that fly-by-night player could step up so masterfully. He never lets me down. He's always there and he always senses right away when anything is bothering me.

Harper keeps going on about how rotten he is. "Did you know he's into some really bizarre stuff? He gets really dark and controlling when he gets turned on. He says all kinds of horrible things. I was really scared of him a few times there. I wonder if any other women in town got on the wrong side of him. Did you hear what Millie Bradford said about him?"

I don't want to listen to whatever every woman in town is saying about Jayden. I usually would block out Harper's malicious gossip, but now I find myself listening extra closely.

Jayden has been a player for years. He never hesitated to do it with any woman that showed an interest in him. He didn't give a damn about their personalities. If they wanted to slum it for a shot at his money, he was more than happy to enjoy their bodies while it lasted.

He's never done any of that with me. He never once wavered in his desire to marry me and he only gets more determined, more support-ive, and more considerate with every passing day.

He doesn't lose interest. If anything, he gets even more focused on us creating a future together. He keeps dropping hints about us having more children and he's completely taken over paying all our bills.

I never would have believed that having a man pay all my bills would make me feel so......so content. I always considered paying my bills a point of pride and accomplishment.

I knew raising Kai alone was stressing me out. I never realized how much until Jayden stepped in and lifted that burden off my shoulders. I actually feel like I can relax and enjoy life for a change. I can be happy, now that I don't have to worry about money every minute of the day.

If we have more children, we'll need a bigger apartment. We might even move to Weeping Willow Lodge. That doesn't sound so outrageous now. It makes sense in a practical, down-to-earth, normal-life way.

Harper starts going on and on about Jayden's sexual habits, but I barely hear her. He hasn't done anything dark or disturbing with me....except for the time he made me admit that I couldn't live without him.

I can't imagine living without him now. I can't imagine living alone and not being able to curl up on his chest with his arm around me.

We still haven't told Kai and Jayden still hasn't officially moved into my bedroom—not in a way that Kai can see. That's the final frontier and it still terrifies the shit out of me. I don't know if I can do it. I thank the stars I have Jayden to make that decision for me. He'll tell me when the time comes.

I get another overpowering flood of gratitude when I think about everything he's done for me. He has stood by me from the beginning. He's gone over the top to make sure everything is okay between me and Kai. Jayden is the reason I still have Kai at all.

I'm grateful to him for so much more, though. This issue of our money is just another reason to rely on him and to move forward with this plan to marry him.

I never thought I'd marry my best friend, but all my old reasons for refusing keep falling away. He hasn't looked sideways at another woman since he first suggested that we get married. He hasn't lost interest in me. He's made me feel like a queen ever since this started.

The waiter comes to take our orders, and while Harper is busy talking to him, I pick up my phone and send Jayden a text. *Do you want to meet me and walk to school to pick up Kai?*

He writes back right away. *I'd love to. I can't wait to see you.* He ends the message with a kiss emoji and then sends through a huge red heart.

My stomach flips looking down at it. I know he loves me and I love him, but this feels different from the friendly love we've always shared before.

Am I in love with him? Thinking that gives me butterflies and makes my heart pound. I can't wait to see him, either. I can't wait to feel his comforting arms around me. He'll protect me from anything. He'll solve any problem that comes our way. I never have to worry about anything when he's with me.

The waiter distracts me and I put my phone away. I can concentrate on supporting Harper, now that I know I'll be seeing Jayden after this.

I listen to her latest tragedy with Ernesto, whoever that is. He sounds like an even bigger douchebag than Jayden—or the way Jayden used to be.

Jayden would never promise to take a girl somewhere for Christmas if he only planned to dump her, but none of that matters because he says he isn't interested in anyone but me.

He doesn't have to tell me that because his actions prove it. He never talks about anything but us and he always comes straight home from work every day. He never goes anywhere except with me and Kai and Jayden always gives us his undivided attention when he's with us.

I get out of the lunch date with Harper as soon as I can. I don't want to waste any more time with anything other than building my life with Jayden. I really want to do this now. I don't want to wait anymore.

It's just the question of telling Kai that holds me back. It holds both of us back. I see Jayden shudder when we talk about it. He's just as intimidated by the idea of telling Kai as I am.

We have to do it sooner or later. Maybe we should decide on that today.

I hurry across town and meet Jayden at the park down the street from the school. We always come here with Kai on the weekends. This is the first time Jayden and I have ever been here alone.

He doesn't smile when I approach him, but that look in his eyes leaves me in no doubt that I'm the only thing on his mind. He puts his arms around me and draws me into a slow, sultry, luxurious kiss.

I collapse into that unbelievable feeling of his hands around my face. His lips carry me away to another world where nothing exists but him.

We're standing in the middle of a public park kissing like lovers because we are lovers. I love him, and in that kiss, I feel the drowning tide of earth-shattering, cosmic love for him. I'm in love with him. I'm drop-dead lost in love with him.

I want the whole world to see me kissing him. I don't care what anyone thinks. I want him. I want him in my life. I want to share all our troubles and trials with him. I want him to take over my life and to discuss all our issues and struggle every day to make this work. I don't want to be anywhere else but right here in the middle of this with him.

He breaks off kissing me and pulls me into a hug. He crushes me so tightly that I can't breathe and I hug him back just as tightly. My heart aches with love for him. Hugging him is even so much better than kissing him or having sex with him. It means we're together. Nothing can tear us apart.

When he straightens up and looks into my eyes, I see it all in their sparkling green depths. What would it mean to say, *I love you?* We already know we love each other and now we're madly, hopelessly in love with each other. What's left except to get married?

He eases back just a little more and takes my hand. "How you doing?" he asks.

I nod. "I'm good."

"You okay?"

"Yeah," I reply.

It's always like this. He constantly checks in with me to make sure I'm okay with everything that happens. He would be all over it if I said something was wrong.

We start strolling through the park toward the school, but we take our time getting there. We have almost half an hour before the bell rings. I don't want to hurry and Jayden doesn't speed things along.

"I was thinking we should tell him," he murmurs. "It's time."

"I know," I breathe back. "Anyway, if we tell him, it means you can finally move into my room."

He glances over at me and blushes. "I wouldn't mind putting it off a little longer and not because of that."

"I know. I'm as nervous about it as you are, but we both know he'll be delighted."

Jayden nods. We both know it. Kai would be ecstatic if he knew Jayden and I were going to get married.

"My mother wants us to set a date," he murmurs.

"I guess that's understandable," I reply.

He pulls me to a stop and looks deep down into my eyes. "Are you okay with that?"

"Isn't that what we've been talking about all this time—getting married? What else is there but to set a date and start planning it out?"

"I know. It's just...." He squints across the park toward the trees. "It's all getting real real quick, you know? Living with you is wonderful. I've never been happier in my life. It's just....so real. There's no going back from that once we do it."

"I don't want to go back and I know you don't, either. I'm as scared about it as you are, but at least we know it will be good." I squeeze his hand. "You know it will be good."

"Yeah." He turns back to delve deep into my eyes. "It already is."

"It can only get better as long as we're together," I tell him.

He pulls me into another hug. It feels heartbreakingly beautiful to be able to share these moments with him. We're doing this together. We're together in every way that counts.

Hugging him like this feels like we're friends. We're friends in ways we never were before because we're committed to our shared future. I can't imagine anything better than that.

All the years we spent as friends only gives us a more solid foundation to build this house, this family, this bridge to the future. It's the best possible experience we could ask for. We can work out anything as long as we have that.

Without warning, Jayden puts his hand in his pocket and pulls out a small black velvet box. He opens it in front of me, takes out a beautiful diamond engagement ring, and slips it onto my finger without asking. He doesn't have to ask.

He holds up my hand admiring the effect the ring has. It feels strange.... but good. It sparkles with the same mysterious power his eyes exert over me every time he looks at me.

Then he kisses my knuckles, squeezes my hand, and we start walking on our way to the school to pick up Kai. He'll see the ring and then we'll have no choice but to tell him.

Chapter 22: Jayden

I turn to face Quinn in front of the school and another colossal crashing wave of love drowns me when I look at her. How is it even possible to love a woman this much?

My heart feels like it's going to crack in its efforts to keep up with how much I love her. The thought of telling Kai that I'm going to marry his mother doesn't scare me anymore.

Okay, yes, it does scare me. It terrifies me out of my wits, but it will be worth it if it means I can finally seal the deal with Quinn. I have to tell him, and as soon as I do, I can move into Quinn's bedroom and take her to the altar and live happily ever after with her. That makes the terror worth it.

I can go through with this when I look at her. She offers me all the living proof I need to know that it's worth it. She would be worth a lot more.

The bell rings, but I pretend not to hear it. I just have to keep looking at her. She loves me. I know it when I look into her eyes. She doesn't smile. She gazes up at me with a mixture of aching desire, fear, and wide-open expectation.

I never thought having her depend on me would make such a difference. She leans on me and follows my lead perfectly. She never balks when I make a decision. She completely relinquished all control of her finances to me exactly the way she said she wanted to.

She seems happier now—not so stressed out all the time. She's much more relaxed now that she doesn't have to worry about money.

I wish I could have spared her eight years of struggle, but she wasn't ready for this then. She would have fought me and it would have ruined us if I tried to take that responsibility for her before now. She's independent. She needed to set that burden aside on her own, not have it taken from her.

I love her for that. I love that she can surrender herself to me in so many ways and she doesn't resent the surrender, either. She embraces it. She loves it. She thrives on it.

She makes me so much stronger. She makes me so much more the man I'm supposed to be. She makes me want to carry and support and protect her. All those things make me love her more—as if I could possibly love her more than I already do.

We just have to tell Kai. That's the last mountain to climb and we'll do it together. We're here together, and in a few minutes, he'll come through that gate. He'll see us together and we'll tell him. Then we can all move forward as a family.

I tear my gaze away from Quinn, but I don't let go of her hand. I need her to get me through this.

We both turn to the gate as the kids come streaming out of the school. I search every face looking for him—my son. I'm his father. I stand at the gate with the other parents waiting to pick up their kids.

Quinn squeezes my hand and an electric charge runs up my arm. This is it. The moment of truth. None of us will ever be the same after this. I want to get it over with at the same time that I want to run away and hide from it.

I break out in a sweat counting down the seconds until he comes out. Kids stream past me. Cars start pulling out of the parking lot as the other parents take their kids home. More and more kids come out....and then the principal comes out.

The crowd starts to dwindle. I rotate from side to side searching everywhere for Kai. He has to be here somewhere.

"Where's Kai?" Quinn asks in a cutting tone. The note of alarm in her voice sets my nerves on end.

I spin back the other way. The flow of kids coming out of the school gets even thinner. Only one or two more kids comes out.

"He should be here," I mutter.

"Kai!" she yells across the yard and the principal turns around.

"He has to be here somewhere." I stride through the gate onto the grounds.

"Kai!" Quinn roars. She splits away from me heading in the opposite direction and then we both pivot toward the principal.

We converge on him and Quinn starts talking fast. "Have you seen Kai? He didn't come out with the other kids. He should be here. He always meets me right here. He can't be missing."

The principal frowns. He's a middle-aged guy with a bald dome and a greying fringe of short hair around his ears. "He was here just a few minutes ago. I saw him in class right before the bell rang."

He heads for the building entrance. I want to go in there and search for Kai, but I'm not sure if I should.

Quinn walks in matching the principal step for step so it must be okay. I go with them, but I don't feel right about walking shoulder to shoulder with the school principal. Who am I, anyway? I'm just Kai's mother's family friend.

No, I'm not. I'm not just that anymore. I'm Kai's father, and if anything happens to him, I'll tear the whole world apart to find the person who did it.

The principal goes back to Kai's classroom and then goes to check the school's rear entrance. The grounds are becoming more and more deserted by the second as more kids and parents leave. The three of us are the last ones left by the time we return to the gate. Kai isn't there.

"I'm calling the Police," I growl and pull out my phone.

Quinn is becoming more hysterical by the minute. "What if he already went home? What if he took the bus by mistake? What if he went with a friend and forgot to tell me?"

"Has any of that ever happened before?" I ask. "Of course he didn't. He wouldn't do that. Something's wrong."

I press my phone to my ear and fight down panic while I listen to it ring on the other end. The principal goes off to search somewhere else. I only have to look at Quinn's agonized face to know I'm right.

Kai would never leave school without telling Quinn. He knew she was supposed to be here to pick him up. The school has a strict bus schedule and the driver makes sure only the right kids get on the bus depending on each day's roster. The school has policies to cover situations exactly like this one.

"911 Emergency Dispatch," the operator chirps in my ear. "Please state the nature of the emergency."

"We need the Police at West Shore Elementary School right away. A boy is missing."

"Have you checked all the boy's usual locations and destinations?" the operator replies. "Children tend to turn up unharmed given time."

I glance over at Quinn. She paces up and down talking rapidly into her phone. "Are you sure he isn't there? Is the door locked?"

Her expression twists. "No," I tell the operator. "He isn't at home and he didn't come out of the school when we came to pick him up. He's definitely missing."

"I'm dispatching Police to the school now, Sir. Please stay on the line until the officers arrive."

Quinn hangs up and compresses her lips tight trying to hold it all together. I put one arm around her and fold her against me while I listen to the silence on the other end of the phone.

"The Police are on their way, baby," I breathe in her ear. "We'll find him."

"I can't live without him, Jayden!" she moans. "I can't survive if anything happens to him."

"I know, baby." I kiss the side of her head. "I feel the same way. He's going to be okay. We'll find him."

"Police officers should be arriving at the school now, Sir," the operator tells me.

I look around and see three squad cars pulling into the parking lot. They don't have their lights and sirens on, but the silence makes them seem so much more ominous than if they did.

I hang up and put my phone in my pocket. The Police officers start walking toward us, but Quinn is so distraught that I can't ignore it.

She keeps turning this way and that, pressing her hand to her forehead, and curling her lips inside her mouth. She's barely hanging on.

I close both hands around her face and force her to look at me. "Listen to me, Quinn. We're gonna find him. He's going to be all right. Understand? We're going to find him. Nothing is going to happen to him."

She nods fast, but looking into my eyes just makes her more upset. I let go of her and put my arm around her shoulders to go meet the Police.

We get there at the same time the principal comes rushing over. "The security cameras......the security cameras.....he's.....the back entrance......"

"Where?" I demand a lot louder than I should have. "Where are the cameras?"

"This way!" He waves us forward and the Police join us on our way to the principal's office.

He leads us into a back room banked along one wall with screens. Each one shows a different angle of some part of the school.

He starts rolling security camera footage of one of the corridors. "I swear I saw him in class less than twenty minutes before the final bell rang," the principal tells us. "He left to go to the bathroom. Look."

We watch the footage of Kai leaving his classroom and heading down the hall. He stops at the school's rear entrance and glances out through the glass doors.

At that moment, three men walk in through the doors. They talk to Kai for a second and then pounce on him as one. They wrestle him to the floor and my stomach turns when I see him kicking and screaming trying to get away from them.

His face turns up toward the camera and his mouth opens in a silent scream. Quinn whimpers and turns her face into my shirt, where she starts sobbing uncontrollably.

I can't even blink. I can't breathe as the guys haul Kai out of the school. The principal switches to a different camera showing the men dragging him down the sidewalk, throwing him into a white, unmarked van, and driving off with him.

"This is all wrong," I mutter. "He didn't go to the bathroom."

"What are you talking about?" the principal asks. "Why else would he be out of class at that time? He's a responsible kid. He wouldn't just walk out for no reason."

"Look." I point to a map of the school posted next to the security station. "He was nowhere near the bathroom and you can't tell me those guys just happened to know he would have to go to the bathroom at that time."

"They could have come onto the grounds planning to kidnap someone and just grabbed some random kid," one of the Police officers suggests.

"Roll the footage back," I tell the principal. "Something isn't right here."

He rolls it back. I have to summon all my willpower watching Kai leave his classroom and walk down the hall. He has no idea what's about to happen.

"There!" I point at the screen. "What is that piece of paper in his hand?"

"Oh, my god!" the principal groans. "It's an office slip."

"A what?"

"We send out slips to each class when we need one of the children to come to the office." He gets to work winding the footage back even farther. "Look. Right there."

He shows us another child going into Kai's class and giving the teacher the same slip. She reads it, calls Kai out of class, gives him the slip, and sends him away.

"He was on the way to the office, but no one in the office ever called Kai," the principal husks. "Whoever did this must have planned to kidnap him in particular. They somehow arranged it so he would leave his classroom on his way to the office so they could snatch him."

The Police officers turn away. "We're going to cordon off the whole school as a crime scene and then we'll need to take statements from all of you."

"You can do that at the Police Precinct," I tell him. "I'm going there now."

I grab Quinn's hand and walk out of the school so fast she has to run to keep up with me. I get out my phone and set to work.

I call Stuart first. He's the Deputy Police Commissioner. "What's up?" he asks me.

"I need you to get down to the Police Precinct right away. I'm on my way to meet you there. It's an emergency."

Chapter 23: Quinn

I pace up and down in a private office at the Police Precinct. At least it's quiet in here, but I can't relax. I can't even sit down until I know that Kai is okay.

The giant glass walls of this office give me a clear view of all the people working on Kai's case. Jayden stands out there with Stuart, Reggie, Reggie's brother, the Police Commissioner, the Chief of Police, and a bunch of FBI agents, two of whom are Jayden's cousins.

Reggie works for the mayor's office and Reggie's brother is the deputy governor of the whole state. Jayden called his people in the instant we realized that someone kidnapped Kai.

Jayden has been out there coordinating with everyone for the last twenty-four hours. I don't want to know what they're doing to try to find Kai. Finding out would probably just make me more distractedly hysterical than I already am.

At least no one is coming to tell me that Kai is dead. I couldn't survive that. I just have to keep pacing this room. My agitation won't let me do anything else. If I sit down or stop walking even for a second, it threatens to destroy the last shred of my sanity. This driving panic might already have destroyed it for all I know.

Jayden breaks off and disappears somewhere. I look around the office and then back out at the people working on the case. A bunch of FBI and plain-clothes detectives work over security camera footage from the school and elsewhere. I don't care what they do as long as they find Kai and bring him back unharmed.

The office door opens and Jayden walks in holding a paper cup with steam coming out of it. He comes over to me, but he doesn't try to stop me from pacing. He follows me up and down the room.

"Here, drink this." He holds out the cup.

"I don't want it."

"You need it. It's chicken broth. You need to take something or we'll be worried about you, too. Just drink it."

I take it and I have to stop walking so I don't burn myself. I blow on the fragrant liquid to cool it and catch a whiff of the smell. It actually makes me hungry.

"We're trying to trace the van that took him from the school," Jayden tells me. "It didn't have a license plate, so the Police are using satellite telemetry to follow it from the school to wherever it went."

I take a sip of the broth. It tastes good and burns a path of fire to my stomach. It actually does make me feel better.

Jayden leans in and kisses me on the temple, but he doesn't say anything else. He doesn't say everything's going to be okay. Nothing will be okay until Kai comes home. My life isn't worth spit without him.

I take another mouthful of the broth and it carries another warm flood of gratitude for Jayden. I couldn't get through this without him. He takes care of everything out there so I don't have to. I don't have to hold it together. There's no way I could.

He kisses me one more time. "I'm going back out there. I'll tell you when we...."

The door opens again and a uniformed Policewoman sticks her head in. "Mr. Aldrich? This just came in for you."

She hands Jayden a package the size of a brick. He scowls at it. "Who would send me something *here*? No one knows I'm here. Who sent it?"

"I'm not sure," she replies. "It just arrived by courier."

She leaves and he tears the package open. The wrapping paper falls away and he opens the box inside.

A single slip of paper sits inside and he drops the box when he lifts the slip out.

$200 million in unmarked bills. Bring it to 450 Port Parkway at six o'clock tonight in exchange for the boy. Come alone. No Police or the boy dies.

I feel my brain starting to shut down in a storm of panic. If anything happens to Kai....

"Jayden...." I choke.

He doesn't hear me. He storms out of the room without a word. He leaves the wrapping paper and the box lying on the floor, and as soon as he gets back out there, the Police, detectives, and FBI guys go into a frenzy.

Police and crime scene people swarm into the office and start firing questions at me. "Did you touch the paper? Did you handle any of the evidence?"

I can only stand here in shock with tears pouring down my cheeks. Someone wants $200 million dollars in exchange for Kai. Why?

They sent that ransom note to Jayden. Someone must have figured out that he's Kai's father and now the kidnappers want a slice of Jayden's money.

I don't know what's happening. The crime scene people work furiously over the wrapping paper and box that the ransom note came in. One of them yells in my ear about fingerprinting me.

Just when I think I might snap entirely, Jayden swoops out of nowhere, grabs my hand, and tows me out of the room.

He parks me in the corridor outside and turns me to face him. He cups my cheeks and moves his eyes right in front of me so I have no choice but to stare into the vast depths of his eyes.

"Listen to me, Quinn," he says again. "We're going to get our son. Understand? We're going to get Kai, but you have to be there. You have to be the first person he sees when we bring him home safely. Understand? He's okay and we're going to get him. Do you understand?"

I nod fast. I don't care what we have to do as long as we get Kai back.

Jayden leads me out of the building to the Police parking lot behind the Precinct. Unmarked cars screech out onto the street and Jayden leads me to a different van.

This one is black and we load into the back with at least ten SWAT guys all armed to the teeth.

They slam the doors and the van burns out onto the highway. "Where are we going?" I ask.

"We're doing what the note said," Jayden murmurs. "We're handing over the ransom money in exchange for Kai."

"But that means...." I glance over at him, but when I see his eyes staring back at me, I don't ask any more questions.

Jayden will handle this. He knows a lot more about what the Police plan to do than I do. I'm so out of my mind with worry that I couldn't think clearly about any of this even if I tried. At least the experts are working on it and most of the guys in charge are members of his family. None of them will let anything happen to Kai.

Jayden must have told them about Helena....and Kai....and everything. They know they're working to save one of their own. Kai is part of their family now.....and so am I. That's why I'm here.

The van pulls over on the side of the road and I realize with a pang that we're down the street from the park. We're back at the spot where I met Jayden before we went to the school.

Jayden stands up in the back of the van, yanks off his jacket, and starts unbuttoning his shirt. "What are you doing?" I ask.

"I told you. I'm going to get Kai."

I stare in mounting horror as one of the SWAT guys stands up and starts fitting Jayden with a bulletproof vest. The guy straps it around Jayden's chest with nothing but his t-shirt between him and the vest.

He gazes down at me with a hard, flinty stare while he buttons his shirt over the vest. "Listen to me, sweetheart. This is important. The note said I had to go alone, so you're going with these guys while I go to the port alone."

"But what if...."

"I'm taking my car and going home to make it look like I got the money from there. Then I'll go to the drop-off in my car."

I'm just about to start screaming at him that he can't go through with this. I can't let Jayden go deal with the kidnappers alone. They'll shoot him as soon as they get their money and that vest gives me an extremely bad feeling.

He bends over and glues his cheek to mine. He kisses me and then keeps his cheek sealed against mine while he whispers in my ear.

"You have to be there, darling. You have to be the first person Kai sees when he gets free. You take our son home. Do you understand? What happens to me doesn't matter. Just take him home. I'm trusting you, Quinn. I'm trusting you to take care of our son. Don't let me down."

He gives me one more kiss and the SWAT guys in the very back of the van kick the doors open. The guy that fitted Jayden's vest hands him a black, locked briefcase and Jayden jumps out. He hits the ground and strides off toward his car without looking back.

I gape at the back of his head, too stunned and horrified to make a sound. He can't be walking away from me like this. He can't be walking off to his death to give Kai back to me.

I gulp down rising despair, but he's already getting in his car, turning the ignition, and reversing out of the park. He drives off without looking at me again.

A second later, the doors slam shut and the van takes off. I can't think. He can't be gone. I can't lose Jayden and Kai both in the same day. I can't be alone in the world. What will happen to me? I'm nothing. I'm a ghost. I'm already dead now that they aren't here anymore.

Chapter 24: Quinn

The van screeches to a halt again and all the SWAT guys leap to their feet. They move so fast and there are so many of them that I can't even tell what they're doing.

They all start checking their weapons and speaking random gibberish into their headsets before one of them throws the door open and they jump out.

They don't *all* jump out, though. Three of them stay behind and slam the door shut again with themselves inside.... plus me. The driver climbs into the back and all four of the remaining guys start working even faster.

They snap orders to each other about arrays and coordinates and a bunch of other stuff I don't understand. They fold up the seats on one side of the van's rear compartment and then fold down that whole side section of the wall.

It folds down into a giant desk with camera feeds coming from multiple directions. The four guys sit down on the seats next to me where they can reach all the controls on their desk.

They control each feed with their instruments. I can't tell what they're doing until my brain switches and the guys start talking about drones.

"Drone 1 in position on the west side," one of them announces.

"Drone 5 moving into position now from the northeast. I got eyes on the drop zone."

"Aldrich pulling in now on Drone 3," another adds.

My chest constricts when Jayden's car pulls in at the port. He parks outside a warehouse and gets out carrying the briefcase the Police gave him.

The wind whips his clothes and hair in all directions. He squints into the dust as he strides across the wide concrete cargo-loading platform to a spot in the very center.

He stands straight and tall peering into the wind and dust. He looks haunted and eerie standing there alone.

"Team Gamma in position," one of the technicians tells his comrades. "Report, Gamma."

A scratchy voice comes from the monitors in front of us. "Gamma in position with line of sight on Aldrich and target zone."

"Team Epsilon, report," the same technician orders.

A different voice replies, "Epsilon in position with line of sight on escape routes 2, 8, and 12."

The technicians go through several more teams and two of the drone feeds show us SWAT teams lining more warehouses surrounding Jayden's position.

My heart stands still watching this. All those guns train on Jayden. Is he going to make it out of this alive?

"Target acquired! Target acquired!" one of the SWAT guys crackles through the speaker. "Victim sighted! Victim safety confirmed! I repeat! Victim sighted and victim's safety confirmed! The boy's all right!"

My eyes well up with tears and I have to shake them away so I can look at Kai coming out of a nearby warehouse. Four masked men surround him and two of them keep their fists clenched on his shoulders, but he's definitely alive and well.

He shoots a terrified glance up at his captors when they jerk him into position. Then, like something out of my wildest dreams, Kai's face breaks into a huge smile of relief and hope when he sees Jayden standing there with the briefcase.

Jayden doesn't move and he doesn't smile, either. He keeps his narrowed eyes on the group. The wind slashes his hair across his face and his jacket whips sideways, but he never flinches.

"Aldrich advancing," one of the SWAT guys reports as Jayden starts walking across the platform toward the kidnappers. They stay where they are in front of their warehouse.

"Line of sight on targets maintained," the SWAT guys crackle through the speaker. "Target still acquired."

"Hold your fire until Aldrich and the boy retreat," one of the technicians orders.

Dead silence falls over the van and my heart stops as Jayden halts in front of the kidnappers and holds out the briefcase. He and the kidnappers exchange a few words and Jayden shakes his head before putting down his arm.

"What is he doing?" one of the technicians snarls.

I want to shut my eyes and turn away when two kidnappers raise automatic weapons and point them in Jayden's face, but he still doesn't back down. He waves at the kidnappers and they finally push Kai to the front.

One of the kidnappers gives Kai a shove and snatches the briefcase out of Jayden's hand at the same time. Jayden pushes Kai all the way behind him so Jayden's big body completely protects Kai from the kidnappers. Jayden keeps his hands on Kai at all times while the kidnappers snap open the briefcase.

My world stands still in that breathless moment. None of the technicians makes a sound as all the kidnappers look down into the briefcase.

Without warning, gunfire breaks out somewhere. All the SWAT guys inside the van and outside it start yelling at the same time and everything on the screens explodes in confusion.

I leap to my feet searching everywhere for Jayden and Kai. I catch one glimpse of Jayden spinning around and grabbing Kai in his arms.

The next second, one of the technicians springs up in front of me. He blocks my view of the camera feeds. "Go! Go! Go!" he bellows in my face.

He pushes me to the back of the van, pops the door, and shoves me outside. I don't know what I'm supposed to do, but it all makes sense when I see Kai running toward me at full speed.

I burst into a dead run. I have to get to him. I have to hold him and feel for myself that he's safe. He yells out, "Mom!" and this feeling of aching relief and agony tears my heart in half.

I spot Jayden running right behind Kai as the whole port explodes in gunfire. I can't see or hear anything except my boy colliding with me so hard he nearly knocks me off my feet and then his arms are around me.

I crush him into me with all my strength. I can't stop screaming into his hair. "My boy! My boy!"

Jayden grabs us both, picks us up, and carries us the rest of the way to the van. He throws us into it, clambers inside, slams the door, and the van screeches away in a cloud of burning rubber.

Chapter 25:
Jayden

The SWAT van skids into place at a random curb and I throw open the back doors. The guys from the van leap out and surround me, Quinn, and Kai with every gun pointed outward.

Two of the men grab me and Quinn. We close Kai between us and the guys march us into a random doorway, up some dim stairs, and push us into a tiny apartment in the very back of the building.

"Stay here," one of the guys tells me. "Don't leave until Lieutenant Richmond gives you the all clear. Understand?"

I nod fast and the guy leaves me, Kai, and Quinn alone in the living room, but only for a second. A minute later, a whole squad of more guys in SWAT gear pour into the room.

They stand guard at the front door, the windows, and every other avenue of entry or escape.

I can't stop my heart from hammering. Gunfire keeps ringing in my ears and I can't seem to breathe right. I keep looking around for someone to come out and attack us, but there's no one here but the guys guarding us.

I turn to Kai and grab the side of his cheek. "You okay? Are you okay?"

He nods fast and gasps out each breathless word. "Yeah! Yeah!"

I hug him and kiss his hair. I can't believe how close we came to losing him. I have to command myself to let him go so he can stand up straight, but he doesn't take his arms away from my waist where he hugs me back.

He feels so fucking good standing here next to me. I never want to let him go and I can't stop kissing his hair. This boy.....my son......I can never lose him. I would be dead if I lost him.

He breaks away and throws his arms around Quinn. Tears pour down her cheeks and she keeps petting him all over and sobbing in relief. I put my arms around both of them. My heart can't stand the strain of how much I love them both.

I feel Quinn shaking with sobs and Kai huddles in the protective circle of both of us surrounding him. He doesn't try to get away. He holds both of us just as tightly as we hold him.

This is my family. These two are my whole world, right here in this crappy apartment. I don't care if we ever go anywhere else as long as we're together.

Quinn and I both unwind our arms at the same time, and without thinking, we turn to each other and kiss each other right in front of Kai. I realize a second too late that I'm doing that and I see the moment of realization snap in her eyes at the same instant.

We stare at each other with our lips touching. Did we just blow our cover without meaning to? The same question crosses shadows her eyes. What are we supposed to do, now that Kai can see us kissing right in front of him?

Quinn recovers first. She sniffs, turns to him, and runs her face across her shoulder before she strokes his cheek. "Are you okay?"

He nods again. "Yeah."

"Come over here and sit down." She takes him into the living room and sits him on the couch. "We saw everything that happened at the school. The security cameras caught everything."

They start talking about everything that happened at the school and afterward, but I can't calm down. I pace around the apartment checking everything, but the SWAT guys are all still on guard. There's nothing for me to do.

I go into the kitchen and open the fridge to find it fully stocked. I take a sandwich wrapped in plastic wrap and a bottle of water over to the couch, sit down on the coffee table, and hand the stuff to Kai. "It looks like we'll be staying here for a while until we get the all-clear that we're allowed to leave."

"What happened.....to those guys.....the ones that took me?" Kai asks. He still looks scared and keeps jumping for no reason.

"I don't know," I tell him. "I guess we'll find out in time. I don't think their chances are too good based on what we heard right before we left the port."

He bursts out in nervous laughter. "Yeah!"

His eyes dart up to meet mine and I get another stomach full of butterflies. I was the first one he saw when he got free. I was the one who protected him from the gunfire. I was the one who got him away from those dirtbags before all hell broke loose.

Now I see it in his eyes when he looks at me. He's my son and I'm his father. All that brotherly stuff we've been doing for the last eight years—that's all finished. We have a different relationship now.

It's my job to protect him and I will never, ever let him come to any harm. I'll always be there to protect him and I'll always be the first person he sees when he needs me.

He lowers his gaze and starts unwrapping the sandwich. I glance over at Quinn at the same time she glances at me. Her expression spasms and her eyes express so much uncertainty and poignant anxiety that I know I have to do something about that, too. That's my job—to take that uncertainty away from her.

"Listen, buddy," I tell Kai. "I have to tell you something. Me and your mom....we're gonna get married.....like a real couple. The three of us are going to be together from now on—for real."

He takes a bite of his sandwich and looks up at me before he glances at his mother. Then he nods and says, "Cool," like he knew all along.

I glance over at Quinn to see her eyes swimming with tears, but she looks happy now. It's done and now we can all move on.

I put my arm around her and pull her in to kiss the side of her head. I feel myself shaking with relief. This day can't end soon enough so we can all get to tomorrow that much quicker.

Kai finishes his sandwich. I keep taking tours around the apartment, but it keeps being just as empty as always except that the SWAT guys are still here. Night falls outside the windows, but they don't slacken their vigilance one bit.

Kai stretches out on the couch and Quinn runs her fingers through his hair until he falls asleep. She gazes down at him in blessed rapture in between casting frightened glances around the living room.

I can't stand watching her anymore. I sit down next to her and pull her toward me. "Come here, baby. You need to get some sleep."

"I know. I just can't calm down."

I ease her down on my chest and drape my arm around her shoulders. "We could be here for a while—days even. We're safe here for now. Try to relax and get some sleep."

She settles down and wraps her arms around my ribs. I feel her start to soften, but right at that moment, the SWAT guys start talking rapidly into their radios and four of them surround the front door, two on each side.

They aim their rifles at the ceiling and stand tense and alert, but they back off when another posse of their buddies enters the apartment. They talk fast and they surround one guy in a black uniform. He isn't wearing a bulletproof vest, helmet, or radio and he isn't armed.

He gives orders to everyone and it's obvious he's the one in charge. The nametag on his uniform reads, *Richmond*. This must be the lieutenant.

He assigns the new guys to take the old guards' places. I wait for a break in the conversation before I approach him. "What's going on? What's the situation out at the port?"

"The port is secured, Sir," he tells me. "Three of the suspects were neutralized and the fourth is in custody being interviewed by the FBI as we speak. We'll be keeping you and your family under guard until morning. If we don't identify any further threats, we'll transfer the three of you to a secondary location and you can go about your business as normal from there."

He goes back to his business and I return to the couch where I sit down next to Quinn. "There you go," I tell her. "Nothing to worry about."

"What secondary location are they going to take us to?"

"I have no idea, but it doesn't pay to worry about it. I guess we'll find out in the morning. Come here, baby."

I pull her back down on me and she collapses with a deep, shaky sigh. She squeezes me and then moves her hand back over to Kai. She rests her hand on his shoulder while he sleeps. Now we're all connected in one seamless whole. Nothing can break that connection.

I close my eyes and lean my head back on the couch cushions. I can rest, now that I have them with me and nothing will separate us.

Chapter 26: Quinn

I wake up when Jayden starts moving around. "Wake up, sweetheart," he tells me. "We're moving out."

I sit up to see a lot more SWAT guys crowded into the apartment. No one can move right or left. There isn't even space for us to get off the couch.

I don't want to leave Jayden's chest. Listening to his heart beating under my ear was the only thing that helped me relax enough to fall asleep last night.

The lieutenant in charge of this operation comes over to us. "We'll be moving you downstairs and transporting you to your secondary location in ten minutes. Please be ready to move when we give you the word."

I turn to Kai. He's already sitting up and squinting the sleep out of his eyes. "What's happening?"

"They're moving us, sweetie," I tell him. "They're taking us somewhere else. We don't know where, but we need to be ready to move."

Jayden gets up and elbows his way through the assembled men. He goes to the kitchen and brings back a bunch of sandwiches, water bottles, and a few pieces of fruit.

He hands them out to me and Kai. Then Jayden sits back down on the couch while we all eat and wait for something to happen.

The SWAT guys get tense and agitated a few minutes before the ten-minute mark. They move around a lot more and then they start organizing themselves into two flanks.

They form a corridor between us and the door. At the stroke of ten minutes, two guys I've never seen come toward us and wave us forward. "Follow us, Sir—Ma'am. This way."

We stand up and the SWAT guys surround us in guns. Jayden and I instinctively close around Kai to block him between us. The SWAT guys hustle us out of the apartment and all the men behind us close in a wider block so we have no choice but to keep going.

We get swept on a wave of bodies out of the apartment, down the stairs, and back outside where they bundle us into another van. The door slams shut and the van speeds off.

Jayden and I hold onto Kai at all costs. He clings to both of us in a death grip and he huddles between us where we can give him any protection possible.

Nothing happens now that the van is racing away through the streets. The SWAT guys stay alert and watchful all the way until the van veers hard around a corner and lurches to a stop.

Jayden and I hold our breath while three of the SWAT guys talk into their radios. I have no idea who they're talking to or what they're talking about.

"Quadrant 4D secured," one of the snaps.

"Quadrant 5G secured," another replies.

"Quadrant 2F secured," the third adds and then they all nod to each other.

The second one turns to Jayden. "It's all secured, Sir. You can disembark."

Two more guys open the back doors and we climb down from the van. My heart stops all over again when I see that we're standing in the driveway at Weeping Willow Lodge. The giant house rises between towering trees that shade the grounds in a leafy canopy.

The sun shines through the branches and dapples on the pavement. Jayden's car sits parked in front of the house. It all looks so peaceful ....so normal.

Kai gasps. "What the......?"

The second SWAT guy climbs down and dips a single nod to Jayden. "We've secured the area and your brother-in-law has posted private security around the property. We'll leave you here for now. You should be safe here. Ma'am."

He nods to me and he and his guys get back in the van before driving off.

I can't believe I'm actually here. Kai keeps staring at everything with his mouth open. "What the holy crap is this place?"

Jayden squeezes his shoulder. "This is where we're going to be staying for a while. We need to do some investigating on the guys that kidnapped you before we're sure you can go back to school and everything without someone else trying the same thing. We need to develop a full security protocol for you, now that you're an Aldrich. You, too, Quinn. If someone did this to Kai for being my son, we can only assume they'll be looking at you as a target, too."

I can't reply. I can hardly believe I'm actually here. Jayden is thinking about our future and keeping all of us safe.

Right now isn't the time to think about any of that, though. He slips his hand into mine. "Come on. Let's go inside and see what this place has in store for us."

We go inside and Kai can't stop gasping and exclaiming over every room, every stick of furniture, the grounds, and everything else.

Jayden goes off somewhere and Kai leaves to explore the grounds. "You'll find a stone wall around the property," Jayden tells him. "You'll see the security guys on the wall so just remember to stay inside that perimeter."

I wander around the house. It's more of a mansion or maybe a smaller castle. It's a toned-down version of Aldrich Estates. I'm not used to a house this big, but I guess that could change after I've been here for a while.

The lodge is definitely safer than my apartment. I don't want Kai setting foot outside the wall until we know it's safe.

I go upstairs searching for a room to call my own. I spent some time here with Jayden when we were kids, but I didn't look around the place thinking I might actually live here someday.

I make it all the way to the third floor before I find what must be the master bedroom. It's bigger than my whole apartment with an elevated level where the bed is, a sunken sitting room all to itself, and a bathroom nearly as big as the whole upstairs of my apartment.

A massive bathtub sinks into charcoal-grey paving stones and looks out over a secluded part of the grounds. No one can see me in here. A curved wall of glass bricks surrounds a wet-floor shower in the opposite corner. There's also a sauna built into the wall.

I go upstairs to see the loft where a gigantic sleigh bed occupies the center. Windows in the gabled roof give a view of the clouds scudding across the morning sky.

I lie back on the bed and gaze through the windows at the clouds drifting past my exhausted eyes. What will it be like to lie here and see the stars overhead before I fall asleep each night?

This house feels normal to me, now that I think that way. I'm still the same person I was in my apartment. Living in this house doesn't make me any less normal. Maybe Kai will be the same way. In fact, I know he will.

I stiffen when I hear footsteps crossing the sitting area downstairs. "Are you in here, Quinn?" Jayden asks.

"Up here." I sit up and decide to stay where I am when I hear him climbing up to the loft.

"This isn't too bad," he remarks. "I thought it would be falling apart after you mentioned my mother renovating it."

"Not too bad! It's stunning."

"Is it too stunning for you to live here?"

"Of course not! It's amazing."

"I'm glad you think so. That apartment would be a security nightmare." He collapses on the bed and stretches out looking through the roof windows the way I just did. "As soon as I contact Stuart about the security arrangements, I'm going to pass out and sleep for a week. Just telling you."

I smile down at him. "Maybe I should sleep in another room so I don't disturb you."

"Don't you dare!" He hooks his arm around my waist and pulls me down on top of him. "You aren't going anywhere ever again."

I laugh, but I stop when we start kissing. He feels so strong and sturdy and solid. This is the man who saved my son from those kidnappers. This is the man who threw himself in front of a gun to save Kai's life.

I'll never stop loving Jayden for that. I never want to be anywhere else ever again, either. I just want to be right here in his arms and feel that I'm the one he protects and supports and takes care of. I can't believe my luck that I finally found him.

Now we're here in the house that will become our home. Our children will grow up here. In time, it won't seem so big. It will feel lived in and well-loved.

I feel my body waking up to this deep desire for him and all the possibilities between us. I rock my hips against him and my passion for him erupts when I feel him getting hard. We need to christen this bed and what better time than now?

His hands glide down to my ass and he sighs when he crushes me against him. I press my breasts into his chest except that he's still wearing the bulletproof vest. He didn't take it off last night.

I sit up and straddle him while I push his jacket aside and start unbuttoning his shirt. He makes a small noise of satisfaction in his throat and shuts his eyes in delicious bliss before he opens them to gaze up at me.

I can't stop beaming at him. I love him so much. He's the best of men. I love every flicker of his facial expressions, every strand of his hair hanging over his forehead, and every caress of his warm, soft hands.

I spread his shirt apart and he groans when he has to sit up again for me to take his clothes off.

He lets me pull his jacket off and then lay aside his shirt before I rip away the Velcro holding the vest in place.

His chest, shoulders, and back don't look right until I take off the vest and see him in his t-shirt. He doesn't stop me from taking that off, too, and when he puts his arms around me and starts kissing me deeper and stronger than before, his heat radiates into me through my clothes.

He lifts me onto his lap and I don't have to wonder where this is going. This is our bedroom. This is where we'll both fall asleep in each other's arms looking up at the stars every night.

He peels my shirt off and flicks my bra open. He lays everything aside and then rotates me onto my back. He kisses me endlessly, and when he pulls off to dive into my neck and creep down toward my breasts, I look up through those windows at the blue sky above.

It soothes all the worries and strain that brought us to this point. It hints at so many pleasures yet to enjoy and he'll be there for all of them. He'll be the one who gives them to me and he'll be the one to guard me so I can enjoy them in peace.

He pushes himself up on his arms while he corkscrews his hips between my legs. Our pants still hold us apart, but that won't last long.

"Before we do that, we have something important to discuss, Quinn," he tells me.

"Is now the time to discuss it? I might not be in the most rational frame of mind to have a serious discussion."

"You're rational enough for this." He lowers himself enough to kiss me some more, but when I put my arms around his neck and try to pull him down, he breaks away. "Don't try to change the subject. You won't get away with it."

I blush up at him. He makes me so happy. "All right. What do you want to talk about?"

"We need to decide on something before we do it in this bed—in this room. We can't do it until we make a decision on something."

"What is it?"

"We need to set a date."

"Tomorrow?" I ask.

He snorts with laughter. "I'm going to roll over and go to sleep right now if you don't get serious."

"I am serious. We can go down to the country courthouse with Kai and get married."

Now it's his turn to blush. "I would love that, but my family would never forgive us."

I close my eyes feeling wave upon wave of blissful desire wash over me. "Whenever is fine with me. I don't care when it is as long as we get married."

He bends down and kisses me for a long time before he lifts off me again. "Your birthday is in October. Let's do it then."

"You mean.... on my birthday?"

"Why not? That will make it easy for you to remember so you don't forget to meet me at the altar."

I burst out laughing and he joins in. Exhaustion, desire, and pure relief makes me laugh more than I probably should, but who cares? We're together. We'll all be together.

"Okay. That will be a wonderful birthday present for me."

"I'll be your birthday present, baby." He lowers his weight on top of me and I feel him tense with volcanic passion.

"Then every day will be my birthday."

Epilogue: Quinn

Harper flutters around me flapping both hands. "Oh, my god, Quinn! You look stunning! You look like a princess! You look like a fairy tale! You're the most beautiful bride ever in the history of the whole world!"

My sister Sandy rolls her eyes at me in the mirror. "Will you tell her to get out of here? I can't finish your makeup if she's constantly in the way."

"Could you do me a favor, Harper?" I ask over my shoulder. "Could you go see if my mom needs any help?"

"Oh!" she exclaims. "Sure. Anything you need."

She leaves and Sandy sighs as she bends toward my face again. "Thank goodness she's gone! I honestly don't know how you stay friends with her, Quinn."

"What time is it?" I ask.

"I'm not sure. Karina! What time is it?"

Karina glances at her phone. "We have ten minutes."

Just then, Kai sticks his head through the door. "Are you ready to go, Mom?"

"Karina says I have ten minutes."

"Jayden just sent me up here to check on you. He says you're already ten minutes late."

I spin around and almost knock Sandy over. "I am?"

"Karina!" Sandy yells. "Did you disconnect your phone from your mobile plan again? Your phone isn't keeping the right time."

"It isn't?" Karina frowns down at her phone. "No, it's right. I swear it is."

Stuart comes up behind Kai and taps his knuckles on the door. "What's the holdup?"

"Oh, my god! I'm late. Jayden is going to kill me!" I hop out of the chair.

"Your makeup isn't done!" Sandy yells after me.

"Who cares? He already knows what I look like." I steal one last look in the mirror and wilt in relief. "I look fine. Come on, Kai."

My sisters scramble to pick up the train of my dress and we hurry downstairs to the inner courtyard of Aldrich Estates. I can hear the organ playing outside on the terrace. At least it isn't playing the bridal march yet.

Eva and Pauline stand there waiting with Mrs. Aldrich and my mom. It's a good thing I can't see the altar from here or I would be a nervous wreck.

The music changes the instant I set foot in the courtyard and everyone lines up while Sandy and Karina arrange my train behind me.

Andrea goes first scattering flower petals across the terrace. Simon goes next escorting Mrs. Aldrich and they disappear out of my sight followed by my mom. My heart starts to race as I inch closer to the terrace threshold. What will I see out there?

Harper goes next followed by Eva and Stuart, Reggie and Pauline, James and Karina, and finally Sandy with her boyfriend, Jeff.

Now it's just me and Kai alone in the courtyard. I look down at him and he beams back up at me. I don't have to ask if he's okay with this. He's been by my side ever since Jayden and I broke the news.

He holds out his elbow and I blush when I take it. It looks like he's been taking lessons from someone. We glide the last few steps to the terrace doors and the organ starts playing the bridal march.

Kai steps out onto the terrace and I see the long pathway of flower petals leading to a floral arch at the far end of the terrace. Chairs line both sides of the aisle with people from both families.

Harper and my mom hold each other in the front row on the bride's side sobbing their eyes out, but I can only see one person on the whole terrace.

A line of men in black tuxes stand on one side of the altar beyond the arch. Eva, Pauline, Sandy, and Karina stand on the other side.

Stuart and Reggie stand behind Jayden, but he eclipses everyone else out of my awareness. We might as well be alone out here.... except for Kai.

I find myself gripping my son's arm as we get nearer to the altar. Jayden's green eyes flash under his hair that falls over his forehead. He nearly drove his mother into an early grave by refusing to cut his hair for the wedding, but I wouldn't have him any other way.

I can't look away from his eyes. This is really happening. I'm about to marry him in front of all our family and friends.

I get so absorbed in looking into his unwavering eyes that Kai has to stop me in the right place.

"Who gives this woman in marriage to this man?" the minister asks.

"I do," Kai replies and a murmur of appreciation goes through the crowd.

Jayden steps forward and grips Kai by the shoulder. "Thank you, son."

Kai goes bright red, but he takes my hand and passes it to Jayden so gallantly that I want to hug Kai and kiss him right here in front of everyone.

I'll have plenty of time for that and I don't want anything to interfere with me marrying Jayden.

To my surprise, Kai turns to me and squeezes my hand one last time. "I love you, Mom."

He rises on his tiptoes and kisses me on the cheek. Tears spring to my eyes and I hear more people sniffing and boo-hooing out in the crowd.

"I love you, too, sweetheart!" I whisper. "Thank you so much."

He smiles at me and retreats over to join the other groomsmen. Stuart pulls Kai into line, turns him around in the place where the best man should stand, and Stuart clamps both hands on Kai's shoulders from behind.

He gives Kai a very gentle shake and now nothing stops me from facing Jayden. I can swim in the vast depths of his eyes all I want.

I barely hear the service except when Jayden turns to Kai and Kai hands him the ring. The rest of the time I stay floating in that blissful sea of green where all my dreams come true. I never want to leave it and now I never will.

The End.

If you enjoyed this book, please consider leaving a review. You can also support me on Patreon at www.patreon.com/InvisiblePublishing.

Sign Up Once--Get all A.E. Moran's free books including brand new releases

When Doctor Lily Rice moves into a small mountain town to live in isolation away from the world, she sets off a chain of events no one could predict. Her arrival throws town doctor Parker Davis into turmoil. Is Lily trying to steal his patients and drive him out of practice.....or is there something much more sinister at work here?

The two get thrown together by circumstance and fate, only for secrets from both their pasts to threaten everything they've worked to build. Can two broken strangers find happiness through devastation before disaster tears them apart?

Sign up at www.authoraemoran.com to read it for free.

About AE Moran

A.E Moran is the contemporary romance pen name for Theo Mann.

I write 70 books per year—and yes, before you ask, all these books are my original creative work. Nothing written under my name is AI-generated or ghostwritten because I write better than AI and any ghostwriter out there.

People don't read fiction for entertainment or to escape from reality. People read fiction to see their humanity reflected in another person's character and story.

This is my promise to you. When you read my books, you'll see your own humanity reflected in the characters and stories. I take this commitment to my readers very seriously. My books are an intimate form of communication between us. I would never disrespect my readers by turning that over to a machine or another writer. This is my bond between me and you as my reader.

I write 20,000 words per day as my daily work output. If anyone with a public platform would like to challenge me to prove this in a controlled environment, feel free to contact me on this website's contact page. How do I do write so much? Find out more on my blog, *Crimes Against Fiction* at www.theomann.com.

I worked as a professional ghostwriter for fifteen years. Now I'm going for the Guinness World Record by writing 700 books over the next ten years and 1400 books over the next twenty years, all originally written by me.

See my website for the full book list. I'm also the author of *Proof for the Existence of God* and the *Crimes Against Fiction* blog.

You can find out more at www.theomann.com or at www.author aemoran.com.

Also by AE Moran (so far)